Th...   ...ere
co...

They turned to flee from the hail of death but instead raced into the path of their cohorts' gunfire. Several survivors fled out the open front doors, but most retreated down the back corridor toward the alleyway.

"Move, grab some hardware," Bolan yelled at Stamp, keeping the Beretta up and ready but holstering the Desert Eagle to have a hand free to gather a brace of MP-5s as he moved over the carnage he had created. Ten or twelve dead Chinese lay in the hall of the club, and he had to leap over the corpses as they obstructed a clear run to the exit. The big detective followed, scooping an Uzi and an MP-5 on the run, training the P-38 on the rear exit.

"We need to get back to the car and get the hell out of here."

MACK BOLAN ®
The Executioner

#224 Call to Arms
#225 Body Armor
#226 Red Horse
#227 Blood Circle
#228 Terminal Option
#229 Zero Tolerance
#230 Deep Attack
#231 Slaughter Squad
#232 Jackal Hunt
#233 Tough Justice
#234 Target Command
#235 Plague Wind
#236 Vengeance Rising
#237 Hellfire Trigger
#238 Crimson Tide
#239 Hostile Proximity
#240 Devil's Guard
#241 Evil Reborn
#242 Doomsday Conspiracy
#243 Assault Reflex
#244 Judas Kill
#245 Virtual Destruction
#246 Blood of the Earth
#247 Black Dawn Rising
#248 Rolling Death
#249 Shadow Target
#250 Warning Shot
#251 Kill Radius
#252 Death Line
#253 Risk Factor
#254 Chill Effect
#255 War Bird
#256 Point of Impact
#257 Precision Play
#258 Target Lock
#259 Nightfire
#260 Dayhunt
#261 Dawnkill

#262 Trigger Point
#263 Skysniper
#264 Iron Fist
#265 Freedom Force
#266 Ultimate Price
#267 Invisible Invader
#268 Shattered Trust
#269 Shifting Shadows
#270 Judgment Day
#271 Cyberhunt
#272 Stealth Striker
#273 UForce
#274 Rogue Target
#275 Crossed Borders
#276 Leviathan
#277 Dirty Mission
#278 Triple Reverse
#279 Fire Wind
#280 Fear Rally
#281 Blood Stone
#282 Jungle Conflict
#283 Ring of Retaliation
#284 Devil's Army
#285 Final Strike
#286 Armageddon Exit
#287 Rogue Warrior
#288 Arctic Blast
#289 Vendetta Force
#290 Pursued
#291 Blood Trade
#292 Savage Game
#293 Death Merchants
#294 Scorpion Rising
#295 Hostile Alliance
#296 Nuclear Game
#297 Deadly Pursuit
#298 Final Play
#299 Dangerous Encounter

DON PENDLETON'S
EXECUTIONER®
THE
DANGEROUS ENCOUNTER

A GOLD EAGLE BOOK FROM
WORLDWIDE®

TORONTO • NEW YORK • LONDON
AMSTERDAM • PARIS • SYDNEY • HAMBURG
STOCKHOLM • ATHENS • TOKYO • MILAN
MADRID • WARSAW • BUDAPEST • AUCKLAND

First edition October 2003
ISBN 0-373-64299-7

Special thanks and acknowledgment to
Andy Boot for his contribution to this work.

DANGEROUS ENCOUNTER

Printed in U.S.A.

What is our innocence, what is our guilt?
All are naked, none is safe.

—Marianne Moore
1887–1972

As a society, we're realizing these days
that no one is safe; everyone is at risk.
When innocents are confronted and struck
down, good men are obligated to strike back.
And I will.

—Mack Bolan

THE
MACK BOLAN®
LEGEND

Nothing less than a war could have fashioned the destiny of the man called Mack Bolan. Bolan earned the Executioner title in the jungle hell of Vietnam.

But this soldier also wore another name—Sergeant Mercy. He was so tagged because of the compassion he showed to wounded comrades-in-arms and Vietnamese civilians.

Mack Bolan's second tour of duty ended prematurely when he was given emergency leave to return home and bury his family, victims of the Mob. Then he declared a one-man war against the Mafia.

He confronted the Families head-on from coast to coast, and soon a hope of victory began to appear. But Bolan had broken society's every rule. That same society started gunning for this elusive warrior—to no avail.

So Bolan was offered amnesty to work within the system against terrorism. This time, as an employee of Uncle Sam, Bolan became Colonel John Phoenix. With a command center at Stony Man Farm in Virginia, he and his new allies—Able Team and Phoenix Force—waged relentless war on a new adversary: the KGB.

But when his one true love, April Rose, died at the hands of the Soviet terror machine, Bolan severed all ties with Establishment authority.

Now, after a lengthy lone-wolf struggle and much soul-searching, the Executioner has agreed to enter an "arm's-length" alliance with his government once more, reserving the right to pursue personal missions in his Everlasting War.

1

The noise of Heathrow International Airport, the largest of the three separate airports that serviced London, filled the air. It had been a long time since Mack Bolan, aka the Executioner, had been in the English capital, but he had no intention of stopping on this trip. He was traveling to mainland Europe by a circuitous route, which necessitated a brief stopover at Heathrow while he waited for a connecting flight.

Bolan hated waiting. It sometimes seemed as if he spent half his life in this mode, but that was okay. He could will himself into a state of deep concentration and absolute stillness that resembled a meditative trance, lifting his senses out of the ordinary, honed to a heightened sense of awareness.

Unless completely unavoidable, the Executioner never used civilian airlines. Not only did he find the waiting frustrating, he was also prohibited from carrying weapons with him because of airport security, and that put him on edge. His senses were always attuned to trouble, and to be unprepared because of what seemed like Hal Brognola's whim...

That was unfair, and the soldier knew it. Brognola probably had a good reason for wanting Bolan to slip into France unnoticed by French authorities or any military personnel who would have been utilized to transport him in the usual manner. It was a "possible" mission, nothing more than a rumor. The current round of jostling for position in NATO meant that the big Fed was wary of stirring up a hornet's nest, either at home or on foreign soil.

So, traveling unarmed until he hit French soil and on a passport that proclaimed him Mike Belasko, an IT technician heading to a computer show in Paris, Bolan found himself people-watching and waiting for his connecting flight. Idly, he wondered if the route booked for him was the result of someone chewing Brognola's ear about expenses. The thought of the big Fed being bawled-out by a desk jockey over a few bucks raised the ghost of a smile.

Wandering into a coffee shop, he ordered a cup, then settled to make the most of the wait by catching up on a few English newspapers. He rarely had a chance to kick back and read up on current world events or to see what the rest of the world thought of the U.S.A.

But now when presented with the chance the soldier couldn't settle into the dull newsprint. There was too much noise and activity around, and after a few false starts he gave up trying to read and sat back to observe the mass of humanity flowing around him. He felt distanced from them, and a brief sadness assailed him. He had spent so long fighting the War Everlasting—a fight that would continue until death claimed him—that he was no longer a part of those he fought to defend, the ordinary, everyday people who just wanted to get on with their lives in peace, without the threat of death from the criminal and political elements who didn't give a damn about democracy or freedom. People who, because of their lack of interest in such matters, were ill equipped to defend themselves or to fight back if attacked. These people needed a defender, and Bolan was such a man.

But it had come at a high price: he had lost almost everyone close to him, and those who remained were at constant risk. Furthermore, he had to exist outside the mainstream of those for whom he fought.

A family, about to embark on its annual vacation, passed close enough for him to hear their conversation. The mother was in her midthirties, with long blond hair and a hassled expression. She held the hands of a boy and girl who were close in age—maybe seven and eight—and who were already bickering over who would get the window seat on the plane. The father, just under six feet with thinning dark hair and a slight paunch, carried the youngest child, who looked to be about three and had her mother's fine blond hair. Her father called her Elyse, and spoke to her in honeyed tones, telling her about his first time on a plane, and how excited he was as a child. The child was smiling and giggling.

Behind the family, among the crowds, a hassled businessman spoke rapidly into his cell phone as he hurriedly wove his way through the crush. Passing the harassed blonde, he caught the young boy with the edge of his briefcase, and the child yelped in surprise and pain. The mother exclaimed sharply, and the father turned swiftly, his face darkening with anger.

Bolan expected an argument to develop, but was pleasantly surprised when the businessman stopped in his tracks and cut off his call. He went down on one knee, apologizing directly and asking the boy if he was all right. The father's face cleared, and he waved away the businessman's apology—"accidents will happen." They parted on friendly terms, smiles on both sides.

It was a small and inconsequential scene, but it brought something home to Bolan. These were good people, and to move among them for a while was a reminder of why he carried on doing what he did; someone had to stand up for honesty and decency.

Suddenly, the waiting didn't seem so bad.

Bolan watched the family make its way toward the check-in desk. Suddenly his experienced eye caught something that made his senses snap into overdrive. A harassed desk clerk was in a heated argument with two men. She was trying to keep them calm, but they were in a state of visible agitation. Both were casually dressed in jeans and windbreakers, but their boots were heavy-duty, and seemed out of place with the rest of their clothing. The hang of their windbreakers also seemed odd: it was a telltale sign that the Executioner knew only too well.

The two men at the desk were thickset, with more muscle than flab on their heavy frames. Bolan, himself of Polish descent, knew that Eastern European, almost Slavic build. Even though he was unarmed, he still slipped off his window seat and exited the coffee shop, moving toward the commotion with a measured pace.

As he approached, he could hear the argument more clearly above the general hubbub of the terminal. Their accents bore out his initial impression. As one of them turned, bristle-cut hair framing a face with a heavy brow, deep-set eyes gleaming with anger and a mouth drawn thin and tight with tension, Bolan was reminded of the Serbs he had engaged in combat in recent times.

A quick glance up revealed that the airline was of Italian origin, and so not directly related to the nationality of the men engaged in argument. What Bolan couldn't figure was how they planned to get past airport security and check in with those SMGs that were hidden beneath their windbreakers.

Heathrow security carried little in the way of hardware— if any—and a random attack and massacre as a publicity grabber for some spurious cause would most likely be successful. It seemed pointless, but who could tell with terrorists? If so, how to stall them, cut down their line of fire?

It was when he came into clearer earshot that the reason for their agitation became clear, and also why they were armed.

"—but I keep telling you, sir, I cannot let baggage be collected—"

"And I tell you, cut the crap and let me pick up the goddamn bag. I have authorization, and it's a simple enough task."

The woman on the desk looked flustered and exasperated. She rolled her eyes and spoke very simply and slowly, as though to an idiot.

"I've already tried to explain to you, sir, that the document you have does not authorize clearance—"

She was interrupted by the other Serb, who asked his companion what was going on. He was answered tersely. "Useless bitch," the second Serb shrugged. It was a gesture Bolan could easily interpret. These men had been sent to pick up a delivery and had been given inadequate authorization by their boss.

The soldier hoped that they wouldn't want to draw any

more attention to themselves, and would leave without any further trouble.

No such luck.

The desk clerk's manager, a reedy-looking man who had been lurking in the background while the beleaguered woman tried to deal with the problem, finally decided to exercise his authority. He strode forward purposefully and spoke in sharp, piercing tones.

"Look here," he began, shaking with either righteous indignation or nerves, "I'd like you to just stop adopting that tone with my staff. I'll have you know that I've called security, and they're on their way right now."

The two men seemingly ignored him, but the soldier caught the glance that passed between them—it was a cold and immediate look that he understood. They had screwed up, and now they might have to blast their way out. He could tell from their frozen expressions that they wouldn't hesitate.

Bolan quickened his pace. He was now only a couple of yards from the edge of the fray. With no weapons, he might be able to take out one of the gunners by hand, but that would still leave one free to start firing. His first target would be the Executioner, and then both gunmen would have the way clear to open up.

He had to distract them long enough to allow people to scatter, but with no authority, there was little he could say to get people moving until the action began. By which time it would be too late. His mind raced as he tried to formulate a plan of action in the space of a few steps.

Then fate intervened, leaving him with no options at all. Things would kick off in a big way, and he was powerless. He drew in a deep breath, preparing to spring forward and sacrifice himself, but even as he began to move he knew it was too late.

The small boy, fretting about his window seat on a plane he was destined never to see, broke away from his mother and hit one of the gunmen on his side, shouting "Hurry up!" It was an undisciplined moment from the child, but the severity of the response was unwarranted. Looking down, a snarl forming on his lips, the distracted gunman hit out at the child with a snarl. The stinging blow caught the boy full in the face, splitting his lip and knocking him off his feet. The father's face distorted in outrage as his wife screamed. He put down his tiny daughter and stepped forward, yelling incoherently and making a grab for the man who had just hit his son.

It was all the gunman needed. Irritated by the screwup and angered by the child, he was now faced with a screaming man.

In one smooth action he opened his windbreaker and clawed for his weapon. It was an Uzi, and the man wielded the Israeli-made machine pistol as if it were an extension of his arm. One tap, and the irate father was drilled with three rounds that showered those near him with blood, splintered bone and shredded flesh.

There was a momentary silence, as the people nearby seemed to freeze before the screaming began and pandemonium broke out.

The desk clerk and her boss both disappeared behind the flimsy facade of the check-in counter. It would offer them little protection, but Bolan could see an open door at the rear of the enclosure. His immediate problem, then, was the crowd in front of him.

They panicked as the second gunman drew his own Uzi and fired a burst across the area to his left. He roared his frustration as he did so, and Bolan immediately learned two things: despite appearances, they were more likely thugs than trained soldiers and mercenaries, adopting a slapdash approach to their escape; and they were both unable to keep their tempers, as they had proved by their actions. He could outthink them, but he was in the open and had no weapons.

His immediate attention was focused on the mother and her children. They stood, immobile, in the immediate vicinity of the gunmen. The blond woman was standing open-mouthed, wide-eyed, staring down at her dead husband. The shock had rendered her completely frozen, and she still held both her daughters, one in each hand. They were screaming in terror, and the son was sobbing, kneeling by his father, whose eyes stared blankly at the ceiling.

Others were scattering and presented moving targets. The gunners seemed to use the spray-and-pray method, and so the runners could take their chances for now. There were already casualties from the first blast, but there was nothing the soldier could do about them.

But he could do something about the stricken family. The major difficulties were that they were split in two—the boy a couple of feet from his mother and sisters—and that they were directly in front of the desk, and therefore the two gunmen.

Alarms added to the shrill screams about him, but Bolan was able to filter it all out and focus on what was in front of him, and the task he had to accomplish. His muscles, trained to a high degree of strength and suppleness, were augmented by a speed of reaction that was awesome, and had been honed by endless combat.

Only a yard or two away, Bolan threw himself forward into a roll. As he came out of it, the leap having carried him that extra yard he needed, he flung out an arm and scooped the boy into his grasp. His arm jarred painfully as the inert weight of the child pulled against him, but his strength and determination allowed him to keep a hold of the child and enabled him to adjust his balance as much as was humanly possible.

The next part was difficult—he had to thrust himself forward and grab the woman and her two daughters, hoping that he would have enough momentum to sweep them off their feet and carry them to safety. He also had to hope that his sudden action would be surprising enough to put off the gunmen for that fraction of a second he needed. If not—and if he was wrong in his assessment of them—then he could expect a hail of lead to rip into his body from at least one of the Uzis.

He crunched into the woman and her children, feeling a bone-jarring clash as his irresistible force met her immovable object. But she was small, and the children were young and still tiny. He had enough power in his heavily muscled legs to drive himself forward hard enough to take them out of the line of fire and into the slender shelter offered by a pillar dividing one check-in desk from another. He felt their speed slow as the extra weight began to tell on their flight, and he willed them that extra inch or two.

There was no need. They cannoned into the flimsy material of a Greek airline check-out desk, the plywood-and-plastic facade cracking and tearing as Bolan's driving dive took them through the facade and past the pillar.

The soldier had been right about the gunmen—they were just thugs, and they were slow. Chips of white paint and concrete ricocheted around them as a hail of Uzi fire ripped up the corner of the pillar and tore into the far end of the shattered facade. The angle was such that the soldier was able to shield the woman and children from the chips, knowing that the gunmen couldn't fire at them directly unless they moved around.

And that they weren't going to do, not when the purpose of the firestorm was to clear a path for their escape.

The woman looked up at Bolan. His eyes were just a few inches from hers, and he could see the shock and fear in them. The boy was crying, a note of pain in his sobs. The girls were mute, their screams stopped by the shock of the impact. Bolan tore his eyes away from the woman's and focused on the door at the back of the check-in cubicle. It was open, and safety for the family lay beyond.

Bolan jumped to his feet and pulled the family toward the door, the mother scrambling to her feet and tugging at her children as she snapped back into the moment and realized what Bolan was trying to do.

The Executioner made sure they were safely past the door and then turned back toward the sounds of gunfire. The commotion had moved down the concourse, and as he surveyed the carnage, his jaw set in anger. Ahead of him lay a scene of devastation. The spray-and-pray, panicked tactics of the two gunmen had cut a bloody swath down the concourse. Paneling and glass were shattered, and the floors were slick with blood as a number of innocent travelers had been hit by the random fire. Some were obviously dead, sprawled on the floor with their lifeblood slipping away, while moans and groans from some of the prone bodies at least spoke of life.

People had been going about their everyday business, families preparing for vacations, heading perhaps for family reunions that would now only happen in a funeral home. It was unnecessary, and an immoral waste of human life.

Bolan thought of the children he had just helped to safety, and of how they would never see their father again, never grow up with his love and presence. And for what? Because a couple of strong-arm hoods had panicked and been angry that things hadn't gone their way?

Hal Brognola's mission could wait a few hours. Mack Bolan had unfinished business here. Maybe airport security and the police could mop it up, but maybe not. If the gunmen had the drop on the security, and they weren't armed, then it would take time for the police armed response units to arrive. Most police in England still weren't armed, and any hardware would have to be handed out to trained officers before they could respond to the threat. Bolan had no doubts about their efficiency, but the very nature of their system wasted valuable time.

The concourse curved sharply to the right. Gunfire could be heard in intermittent bursts. Small-arms fire was mixed in with bursts from the Uzis, and Bolan guessed that the airport security had some hardware and was returning fire, perhaps trying to contain the gunmen until the police arrived.

Bolan very rarely allowed personal feelings to influence his judgment during combat, but this situation was slightly different. If he could help nail this scum, then so much the better.

The Executioner took off at a run, his suit jacket flapping as he picked up speed, surefooted despite the blood-slick floor. He covered the distance swiftly, slowing as he neared a curving turn in the concourse. The clear acrylic material of the concourse walls, looking out over the airport itself, should have given him an unobstructed view of what was going down, but it was starred by the random firing of both sides of the battle, leaving the view distorted.

Ricochets of small-arms fire brought the soldier up short as he hit the bend. Dropping flat on the floor, he now had a clear view of the concourse ahead. The gunmen were heading for the nearest exit, which was presumably the one by which they had first entered the terminal. Not that they were going to just shoot their way out. They were pinned down momentarily, taking shelter in the open front of a "sock shop," the racks of hanging merchandise destined never to be fit for wear, torn to ribbons by the exchange of gunfire. The security team, about eight strong, was positioned near the automatic exit doors, covering the only way out.

It looked as if the gunmen were doomed. If the airport security could hold the exit until the police arrived, and more security could pursue along the path of the massacre and cut off a retreat, then the men would be trapped where there were no civilians. The sound of distant gunfire had sent people fleeing toward the nearest exit.

From his vantage point, Bolan could see that the gunmen were taking time to reload. Both had been relatively sparing with their fire, for which the Executioner was thankful. They had to be carrying a limited amount of ammo. Otherwise the death toll would have been higher. As Bolan watched, both men, exchanging heated shouts in Serb, were ramming new clips into their Uzis, which left them vulnerable for a second.

It was an opening—not much, but enough. The soldier leaped to his feet and grabbed two pieces of hand luggage. One was a briefcase, and the other was a suitcase that was so overfilled it became a tightly packed hard rectangle with protruding and sharp edges. He scooped them both with his right hand, as they lay to that side, transferring the grip to his left in one fluid motion as he swung his arm to throw the briefcase at the gunman who was about to reload.

His aim was diverted by the sudden sound of a gunshot, and the sudden rush of air that plucked at the arm of his suit jacket. The soldier felt a sudden stinging burn that could only mean that one of the airport security men had fired at him, thinking him part of the offensive, and the shot had grazed his lower arm.

Bolan didn't care about his own minor wound. It was the consequences of the shot that troubled him, the way in which it caused the briefcase to fly just to the right of its intended target, so that it knocked over a display stand but left the gunman untouched. The Serb turned rapidly, ramming home the clip and firing a burst at Bolan. Forced to drop the suitcase before he had a chance to pitch it at the other gunman, it was all the soldier could do to roll into the cover supplied by a pillar before the SMG burst chopped up the floor where he had been a moment before, scattering concrete chips from the pillar.

The soldier cursed. Obviously, an overexcited or overzealous security man had taken it into his head that there were now three gunmen and fired on Bolan as he came into sight, regardless of the fact that he was unarmed and had been attempting to disarm one of the gunmen as the security officer's shot had been fired.

That one reckless shot had made things much worse. Both Serbs were back in the game and rearmed.

Bolan felt a cold gnawing in his gut as he realized the gunmen now had a hostage. He hadn't seen her before, and neither had the Serbs. The shop manager had been hiding behind a counter, keeping silent and still in her terror, probably hoping that the gunmen would move on. But she had seen them reload, and the sudden violence of the blast directed at Bolan had caused her to scream involuntarily, making her a prime target.

She rose from behind the counter and tried to melt into the wall, hoping in her fear that she could somehow pass through it. Her mouth opened as wide as her eyes as one of the gunmen swiveled, training his weapon on her. He almost drilled her with one tap, but a cold, sly grin spread across his face. Shouting something to his companion, he took one step toward the rear of the shop and grabbed her. She gasped, her paralyzed vocal cords unable to produce anything more, and moved woodenly as he pulled her toward his companion. The second gunman returned the grin and nodded briefly.

Holding the woman in front of him as a shield, with his SMG to her temple, the Serb stepped out. She was a tall brunette, dressed smartly and wearing high heels, so she was a level height with her captor, ruling out the possibility of a clean head shot.

"Hey, stupid bastards, stop firing, yeah?" he yelled in heavily accented English. "It's her you going kill, not me."

The smattering of small-arms fire halted. Bolan could feel the tension in the security ranks only too well: it was mirrored by his own churning gut and racing mind. Somehow he had to separate the woman from the gunmen—that would be the only way for them to be taken down. As it stood, there was no chance of his being able to take them on while she was at risk.

"Let her go. There are more armed police on the way. You haven't got a chance," yelled one of the airport security men.

Bolan groaned inwardly. Had these people never been trained in a hostage situation?

The Serb laughed. "You think we going to stick around for that? Now let me tell you what we going to do—me and my friend, we going to walk right through you, get in a car and drive away. Unless you want the woman to die. Now we move."

The gunmen were in a hurry and didn't want to give the security forces a chance to think about their options. Obviously the gunmen weren't about to throw away their advantage by killing the hostage, but they didn't want to give their opponents time to work that out and contain them until backup forces arrived.

Bolan cursed as the second gunman slipped out from cover, his Uzi also trained on the woman's head. He moved in beside his companion, and the two of them took an arm each, their Uzis against the woman's skull. They betrayed enough of themselves to allow a good shooter to pick them off, but in so doing, the reflex would be enough to tap a burst through the hostage's skull.

Without waiting for an answer from the security force, the two gunmen moved forward. They were totally vulnerable at the rear, but Bolan had no weapon with which to take them out, and no other way of tackling them without endangering the woman.

Come to that, how would he get past the security force that had already fired at him in error and panic? The soldier hadn't come this far to let the bastards get away.

Then, when he least expected it, the chance of getting past security unchallenged was given to him.

"Move back—let them pass." The order came from the head of airport security, and was presaged by the sound of sirens in the distance. The police armed response unit was nearing, and the area was most likely being closed down. The airport security officers, out of their depth, were only too happy to hand the matter over to the forces of the law.

"Back right off, or she dies," yelled the Serb who had seized the woman.

"Please..." she pleaded, adding a tiny, terrified voice to the chaos.

It was unnecessary—the airport security force had already decided to grant them safe passage out of the terminal. For the Executioner, there were only two questions—first, would the police arrive before the gunmen could hijack a vehicle, and second, could he get through the security cordon in order to follow?

The latter question was answered simply. The airport security, in its eagerness to be rid of the gunmen so that they would become someone else's problem, had pulled back far enough for Bolan to begin following the Serbs without anyone noticing. As for the former, a number of cars had been left outside the terminal when the firefight had erupted. Several still had their engines running, as their owners had abandoned them and sought cover elsewhere. The Serbs opted for a black BMW sedan with tinted windows. It was a powerful car, yet not so powerful or unusual so as to not blend with the surroundings during a chase.

Speaking rapidly to each other, the gunmen separated when they reached the vehicle, the first man diving low through the open driver's door. He grunted his satisfaction, and Bolan heard the ignition grind before the engine fired into life. A few words were exchanged before the second gunman slid into the passenger seat, still holding the terrified woman as a shield.

The soldier kept low and moved fast and silently. Attention from all parties was focused on the BMW, so it was easy for him to move forward unobserved. He was determined to take another car and follow the Serbs, just on the chance that they might manage to avoid the approaching armed response unit, which was still battling with the ring-road system of the airport and traffic that was as busy as ever.

The Executioner was almost at the entrance to the terminal when something happened that changed everything. From his vantage point, he could see only too clearly the grim expression on the gunman's face as he loosened his grip on his hostage. Without so much as the blink of an eye, the Serb tapped the trigger of his Uzi twice, the first burst of rounds writing a ragged line up the woman's body, bursting blood, bone and flesh out the back. The force of the shots threw her backward, lifting her off her feet. The second burst kept her in the air, jerking her already dead body in a brief dance of death.

The BMW was in motion, the passenger door slamming shut and the tires screeching on the pavement, before the shattered corpse hit the ground.

Bolan was already out of the terminal entrance, his eyes scanning the vehicles immediately outside the doors for something suitable. He found it: a Jaguar XJS, a more ostentatious and so more easily traceable vehicle, but one of a comparable power and size to the BMW. And that was important. He was determined not to lose track of the Serbs.

He threw himself into the vehicle through its open door, ignoring the shouts directed at him from the airport security. A volley of small-arms fire rang out, and Bolan wasn't sure if some of it was directed at him. No matter. It was too late to worry about that right now.

The car's owner had obviously ditched the vehicle when he or she heard the gunplay in the terminal. The keys were in the ignition, and the soldier gunned the engine into life, slipping the car into gear and roaring after the Serbs.

Following them onto the roads that led out of the airport proper, he threw the car into a brilliantly lit tunnel, the sound of the traffic amplified, the whine of the BMW and the Jaguar engine pushed to their max becoming almost overpowering.

The wails of the police vehicles' sirens bounced along the tunnel walls as the emergency response team threaded its way through the normal traffic flow. The BMW and the Jaguar weaved their way in and out of the traffic at tremendous speed, and a collision seemed imminent as the BMW began a long run of passing a line of traffic, speeding down the opposing lane. At least, Bolan hoped it would be imminent for the Serbs.

No such luck. The BMW played chicken with the leading police vehicle, swerving at the last moment to squeeze between the police and the wall barrier on the side of oncoming traffic, sparks flying as metal screeched on metal, taking off the BMW's matte-black finish.

The oncoming traffic screeched to a halt, causing a backup and enclosing the police vehicles, preventing them from turning and following in the enclosed space.

Bolan was the only one who would be able to keep tabs on the Serbs now. The soldier focused his attention on the road ahead. The traffic was deadlocked, but there were narrow spaces through which he could, conceivably, negotiate a path. It would mean slowing and letting the Serbs get farther ahead, but there was nothing else he could do. He dropped a gear and slowed as little as possible, weaving between the two lines of traffic until he made it out the other end of the tunnel.

Getting back to the correct side of the traffic flow, he had a clear run ahead of him. He could see the BMW, now made distinctive by the long scrape on its side, as it negotiated a roundabout the wrong way and headed toward the Great West Road.

Bolan accelerated and took the roundabout directly across the middle, knowing where he was headed. He gained a few seconds that way and was able to track the BMW as it slowed to move among the late-afternoon traffic.

They were headed for the center of London, presumably back to their boss and any safety he could provide. It seemed an insane thing to head into the city when the description of the car would be circulated by now. But then again, black BMWs were common enough in London, and just maybe they could hide in plain sight long enough to get to safety. Whatever, the perps were in his sights, and all the Executioner had to do now was to keep them in view until they reached wherever their destination.

2

Bolan cursed. He had just braked sharply to avoid a motorcycle courier and the driver had turned and given the soldier the finger before weaving his way through the almost stationary traffic. As he moved, and so cleared Bolan's line of vision, the BMW had vanished from the junction, and the traffic signals had turned to red. If the courier hadn't chosen to shoot out from a side street with no concern for the oncoming flow of traffic, then Bolan would have been able to see which road—left or right—the BMW had taken. As it was, he found himself four cars from the junction, halted by the signals. By the time the Jaguar was in position to see either side of the junction, the BMW would be long gone, masked by the constant flow of slow-moving, heavy traffic.

It was all the more frustrating as he had managed to keep them in view for so long. The Great West Road had fed into the West Kensington and Earls Court areas of London, where the roads were old and definitely not built for such a volume of vehicles as now tried to make their way through the busy residential districts. The pace of the vehicles—Bolan always keeping a few cars between himself and the Serbs—had slowed to a crawl, and if he had been armed, it would have been easy at times for the Executioner to leave his vehicle, take out the Serbs with a minimum of risk to passersby and then lose himself in the crowd. But he had no weapons, and the only way to avoid endangering the public was to trail the rats back to their nest and plan their demise from that point.

What he hadn't reckoned on was the crush and gridlock of traffic as the vehicles hit the center of London, moving through Chelsea, past Victoria and Westminster, and into the heart of the West End. From past experience, the soldier knew that the district of Soho was home to organized crime in London, and so it came as no surprise that the Serbs were headed to that area.

The traffic slowed to a crawl, sometimes halting for several minutes. Bolan kept the BMW in view—and then he encountered the courier from hell, pushing out and making him lose sight of the BMW at a crucial point.

Bolan left the Jaguar's engine running, but slid out of the car and jogged toward the traffic lights. They were still on red, but that didn't stop angry shouts and the furious honking of car horns from behind the Jaguar, as other frustrated motorists were bewildered by his actions. The soldier ignored them as he reached the junction, scanning to the left and right.

He caught sight of a black BMW turning left, about 150 yards down the right fork. It had tinted windows, so the interior was opaque...but the scrape of bare metal down one side was a giveaway.

There would be no time to follow in the Jaguar, as he would be caught in the snarl of traffic. Leaving the vehicle in the line of traffic behind him, Bolan set off toward the side street where he'd seen the BMW disappear. He wove his way through the people on the sidewalks, a mix of residents, tourists and shoppers, after the fashionable clothes and music emporiums, the high-class restaurants and the low-rent strip joints and sex supermarkets that jockeyed for attention behind the neon-lit facades. It was still daylight, but Soho had the unreal air of night about it, even now.

As a result, the crowded sidewalks were full of people who were distracted, and either couldn't or wouldn't get out of the way of the oncoming soldier. Progress was quicker than by car, but only just.

Bolan turned down the side street, the glamour of the main drag suddenly replaced by tired red brick and scraggy London pigeons feeding on discarded takeout food. They scattered sullenly, flying up in his face as he increased speed and ran through them.

It was a short road—an alley that led to another main road—and in the time it had taken him to sprint the length, the BMW had crossed over the main road, cutting through the traffic on either side, and had vanished into another labyrinth of side streets.

Knowing that the chase was almost certainly lost, but unwilling to just give up, Bolan found himself slowed by the mass of people thronging the sidewalk he emerged onto. Threading through them, he then had to dodge around the slow-moving traffic on the main road. It wasn't moving at any great speed, but the frustrated drivers were unwilling to stop for even a second to let a pedestrian past, refusing to give up the extra few feet of space they could traverse in that short time. A white Vauxhall coupe nosed at Bolan angrily, the face of the red-haired driver contorting into ugly fury as the silver trim brushed Bolan's thigh. The soldier leaped onto the hood of the car, giving the driver further cause to curse as he nimbly took two steps across the vehicle to land once more on the sidewalk.

He was across and into the maze of Chinatown, a part of Soho that he knew only too well. There was no sign of the BMW in the immediate vicinity, and slowing to a brisk walking pace, the soldier scanned every street he passed, trying to get a lead.

When he did, it was one that left the trail cold. Down a narrow alleyway, with barely enough room to squeeze the vehicle, a truck was unloading stock for a delicatessen on the main road. The tail of the truck was down, and Bolan could see the hanging sausages and salamis, the crates of cheeses...more importantly, he could see the BMW parked at an angle across the narrow road, driver and passenger doors wide open, the vehicle deserted.

The driver of the delivery truck came out of an open door at the back of one of the buildings, casting a bemused glance at the discarded BMW.

"Hey, you didn't happen to see where the driver went, did you?" Bolan asked, hailing the delivery driver as he approached.

The man—thickset, Greek or Turkish, and in his late twenties—glared at Bolan. "No, I didn't," he snapped in a heavy London accent. "But they'd better get back quick, or I'm gonna be stuck here."

"So you weren't back here when the car pulled up?" Bolan continued, ignoring the driver's hostile tone.

"You think I'd let 'em block my way if I was?" the driver

replied with belligerence. "I'd have told them what they could fuckin' do with their beemer, stopping me working. I've got other deliveries—you tell them that," he continued peevishly.

"I will—if I catch up with them," Bolan said as he jogged around the side of the truck.

"Hey! What am I supposed to do about this, then?" the driver yelled after him, gesturing to the BMW.

Bolan turned back. "Move it yourself. See if they've left the keys in the ignition. Anyway, I'm sure you know how to hot-wire a car. You look like you would," he added as he continued on his way.

The truck driver looked after the departing Bolan, unsure as to whether or not he was being insulted, before shrugging and turning toward the BMW. As it happened, he knew very well how to hot-wire a car, but that didn't mean he wanted people telling him he looked as if he did.

Bolan reached the end of the alley and came out into the teeming melee of Chinatown. It was as well for the truck driver that he had been inside when the BMW had been halted. If he had been in the alley and had the same attitude as he showed Bolan, then there was little doubt that he would be little more than a smear of blood and flesh across the pavement. At least that was one less innocent bystander to their account.

Looking around, it became obvious that Bolan had lost the Serbs. They could have gone in any direction, and the heaving mass of humanity that crowded the early-evening streets made it impossible to try to pick them out, even assuming that they were still in view.

It wasn't often that the trail went dead on the soldier, but just when it seemed he would have to give up and try to get back to Heathrow for his connecting flight, fate threw him a curve ball.

"...so maybe those assholes have taken it into their heads to come back. So what? It can be dealt with."

The snatch of conversation that caught the Executioner's attention would have meant nothing to most of the passersby who came within earshot. It could have been an ordinary dispute about business in Chinatown, but to Bolan it carried a deeper meaning—for not only could it be related to the Serbs he had trailed, but also the speaker had a San Francisco accent.

Slowly, the Executioner turned his head, seemingly deciding which direction to walk, like any puzzled tourist. He located the source of the voice: two Chinese Americans turning off the main street and heading back from the part of Soho that Bolan had just left. One was over six foot tall, with long black hair tied into a ponytail, and a gut forming to give lie to the muscular set of his shoulders. The other—the man who had spoken—was a couple of inches shorter, and of a more slender build. But he was whipcord thin, and the way he carried himself suggested a high-tension wire about to snap. His short hair was dyed blond, and was gelled into spikes.

There wasn't much chance of losing that pair, nor was there much chance of mistaking them. Bolan had seen them before, in New York. They worked as enforcers for a triad mob, and their presence in London caught his interest.

The Executioner turned and followed at a distance. Even in the crowds, there was little chance of losing sight of such a distinctive duo, and in the less crowded areas he was able to drop back a little and put some distance between himself and the two triad hardmen.

They walked with purpose through the streets of Soho, ignoring the come-ons of whores and the blandishments of the doormen trying to lure customers into strip joints.

Finally, they came to a recessed doorway that opened onto a flight of stairs, carpeted in red, that led to a well-lit lobby at the bottom. They turned into the doorway and hurried down, disappearing into the lobby. Bolan walked past the entrance slowly, taking a sideways glance inside. The walls and ceiling of the stairwell were lit by fluorescent lighting, and were painted a reflective white. Recently painted, by the look of it.

Bolan walked to the next corner, then looked back along the row of shops and doorways. There was no sign above the doorway itself, and it was next door to a Greek restaurant on one side, and a boutique specializing in metal jewellery on the other. The shop facades led up to neo-Georgian designed house facades, with the windows covered by net curtains or blinds. There was no sign of life visible.

Figuring that the best way to recon the area would be to take it head on and play the tourist, Bolan walked back toward the recessed doorway. As he approached, two overweight men in business suits, looking as though they'd already imbibed their fair share of alcohol, came from the opposite direction and turned into the doorway, loudly laughing as they went.

The soldier raised an eyebrow. Unless they were exceptional actors, they could only be exactly what they appeared...suggesting that the doorway held little danger.

Still wary, but feeling a little more relaxed, Bolan followed the two men down into the lobby. A bouncer in a black polo neck sweater stood by a soundproofed door, with a young blonde barely wearing a dress seated at an overly ornate table. The two businessmen handed over some cash, and the doorman opened the soundproofed door, letting out a wave of heat and the tinny sound of a prerecorded tape of dated disco.

Bolan couldn't help a wry grin. He hoped for his marks' sakes that they were in this cheap joint on business. He approached the table and got an admiring glance from the blonde as she looked him up and down.

"You a member, love?" she asked in a squeaky voice.

"No, ma'am," the soldier replied, softening his voice and adding a vaguely nervous tremor, as though a tourist at large. "But I'm looking for a little action," he added shyly.

The blonde's smile was part indulgence, part vulture as she said, "You'll get plenty of that here, dear, but you'll have to become a member for that."

"I'm sure that'll be no problem," Bolan said, taking out his wallet and making sure both the blonde and the bouncer got a good look at the cash that filled his wallet. "But I'm afraid I haven't had a chance to exchange any since I got here," he added. The cash was in U.S. dollars, to be exchanged when he reached France.

"It certainly won't," the blonde said, taking a handful and counting it out. "We can get it changed for you, no problem. I'll just take it at the current exchange rate," she added, without mentioning what that might be. She handed Bolan back less than half of the notes. "That should see to it, love. Let him in, Chaz..."

The bouncer grinned at Bolan's supposed stupidity as he held the door open. The soldier kept a straight face until he was past the entrance to the club and into the darkness and noise. Then he laughed quietly. By his own reckoning, the blonde had taken him for about 250 dollars, not a large wad of the cash he carried, but more than enough at the exchange rate as far as he was aware. He knew that they would try to take the rest of the money off him by degrees the longer he stayed in the club, leaving him broke.

The funny part was the lack of guile with which it had been done. If the triad enforcers were here on business, then they had a lot of work to do to bring this little branch of the racket up to scratch.

The soldier paused, looking around in the semidarkness to which his eyes were becoming accustomed. The cellar was small, with a raised podium stage in the middle. From somewhere above it came both the rhythmic blast of the music and the garish lighting. A series of polished metal poles ran from the floor of the podium up into the ceiling, and from one of these a young woman hung upside down, swinging around by a hooked leg that ended in a red stiletto shoe. Her short, dark hair waved in time with her moves, and other than a G-string, she was naked. As he watched, she righted herself gracefully and danced out of the pool of light and into the audience. Targeting one of the paunchy businessmen Bolan had followed down, she began to lap dance for him as he smiled like a gleeful child.

Bolan looked away from the spectacle and took in the rest of the club floor. There was a bar along one wall, staffed by a bored-looking topless bartender, her dyed black hair only accentuating her pallor. A man in a rumpled suit, lean and maybe in his late thirties, stood at the bar, nursing a Scotch whisky and trying to engage her in conversation. The other customers were seated at tables that dotted the floorspace. It was still early in the evening, and trade wasn't exactly booming. Apart from the two paunchy businessmen, three other tables were occupied by single men—one of whom had a female escort who screamed hooker—and two that had two men. One of these tables was occupied by the triad duo, the other by two businessmen not unlike those Bolan had followed.

More interesting by far was the only other occupied table. A late-middle-aged man with swept-back gray hair and a designer suit sat listening to a seedy-looking, poorly dressed man with a lined face. He seemed to be pleading with his listener. Two younger men in flashy suits—obviously enforcers—sat back, looking amused at the seedy man's efforts.

There was no sign of the Serbs, but that had been too much to hope for. Bolan looked around for any heavies actually working security for the club, but none was apparent. He wasn't sure if that was a good sign. Without being too obvious, he scanned the room for security cameras locations, but it was too dark in the recesses to be sure either way.

The triad enforcers looked as if they were waiting for someone: so Bolan would wait. He had the time now. Without giving them another glance, he walked over to the bar.

"Jack Daniel's, no ice," he ordered from the bored bartender. She gave him a desultory smile as she measured the spirit and put the glass in front of him. He offered her a couple of bills from his wallet, and resisted the temptation to smile as she gave him a genuinely puzzled look. "The lady on the door said it would be fine," he added, with a barely stressed irony on "lady." The bartender seemed to suddenly understand, and took the bills, giving him a few coins as change that would make it the most expensive drink he'd ever bought.

He turned his back to the bar and leaned back on his elbows, seemingly a relaxed tourist taking in the views—and quite some view, as the lap dancer had returned to her pole and was executing a move of no little acrobatic skill. The Executioner felt his combat sense twitch, that sixth sense telling him he was being watched. He turned his head and saw that the guy in the rumpled suit was staring at him. Catching Bolan's eye, he nodded, smiled briefly and diverted his attention to the dancer.

He didn't look the type for security, and there was nothing about him that pegged him as an enforcer, yet he didn't seem to be in the club for entertainment purposes. That made him a possible danger.

Bolan moved away from the bar and took a seat at one of the tables, trying to get as much space between him and the rest of the clientele as possible. He wanted to be in a position where he could see most of the other customers. As he settled into his seat, a door to one side of the bar opened and closed quickly and a redhead slipped out of the darkness and walked toward him. Perhaps *walk* wasn't quite the word, he noted. She swayed on high heels, her hips rolling, her eyes cold.

He should have figured that they would put someone on him, try to bleed his innocent-tourist persona dry. That was a problem. He didn't want to be burdened with her or be distracted.

Bolan kept his attention focused on the tables at the far side of the club, where the triad duo sat impassively, and the seedy-looking man was getting desperate in his pleas. He was almost at the point of sinking to his knees, it seemed. The redhead, in a fake silk sheath dress whose powder blue clashed with her hair, moved across his line of vision, and in that fraction of a second, the emphasis in the room changed.

For when she had passed and sat next to Bolan without

invitation, the Executioner could see that the triad enforcers were no longer as impassive. Their attention was now directed toward the seedy-looking man, the enforcers and the guy Bolan had tagged as a mob boss. They were still laid-back, but it was pretty obvious that something—obscured from his view by the redhead—had happened. One of the enforcers had moved, and had the seedy-looking man by the hand. He was grasping the man's pinkie, and bending it back. It was extremely painful for such a simple move, and the enforcer's victim was arching back in his seat, his arm and spine trying to follow the line of his forced finger, as though that would help the agony.

"You looking for some company tonight, sweetheart?" the redhead asked him.

"Yeah, mebbe," he answered noncommittally, not even looking at her. Taking this as a definite yes, the redhead signaled to the bartender, who loaded a tray with two glasses and a bottle of cheap champagne, and brought them over.

Bolan ignored this, his attention focused on the scene now unfolding. A glance around the club revealed that the lone table customers and the two pairs of businessmen were still engrossed in the floor show. The guy at the bar, however, seemed as interested in the events at the table as Bolan was.

The middle-aged man in the designer suit asserted his authority by raising his hand. The enforcer let go of his victim's finger and the man tumbled off his seat.

As the man got up off the floor, he looked across the room and for the first time saw the triad hardmen. A look of complete astonishment, followed by relief, crossed his face. Bolan stared at the triad enforcers, and saw the leaner of the two shake his peroxided head almost imperceptibly. The seedy-looking man's expression changed from gleeful to crestfallen. He turned sharply and said something to the suit and his enforcers.

Bolan felt the hooker at his table prod him on the arm, having poured two glasses of the cheap champagne. He moved his arm out of reach, tensing in his seat. He didn't have to pretend to be a tourist anymore. This was going to kick off at any moment.

The slick suit gestured at his enforcers, whose hands shot in unison under their jackets for concealed holsters. If shooting began, Bolan would once more be at a disadvantage.

But, to his surprise, the men didn't pull guns from beneath their jackets. Both sprang to their feet pulling razor-sharp machetes from their sheaths, the edges glittering where they caught the light thrown out from the podium. They adopted combat stances as the triad hardmen rose with breathtaking speed and flung themselves forward. Bolan was expecting them to pull out some hardware and blow away the opposition. To his further surprise, they chose to take on the enforcers with only their martial arts skills.

There had to be a reason why they chose not to use hardware, but now wasn't the time to wonder about it. Bolan noted that the other customers in the club were now aware of the growing altercation, and were reacting with varying degrees of fear. Some were frozen, others blustering...and the guy at the bar stayed calm, just watching. He was cool; Bolan had to give him that. He was just curious as to what was on the guy's agenda.

The bartender had disappeared, and the hooker who had been at one of the other tables was also making a break for the bar. Bolan's unwanted companion also raced for cover. On seeing the machetes emerge, the pole and lap dancer had stopped gyrating and had screamed. She was rooted to the spot as the fight began.

Bolan was inclined to let the hardmen kill off one another, and then just mop up. But it wasn't that simple. There were innocent bystanders, and he'd seen too many get hurt already on this day.

The seedy-looking man was caught between the four enforcers, and he looked around, trying to work out his best escape route. As he tried to dodge toward the door at the back of the club, by the bar, he was knocked unconscious by a blow from the blunt hilt of one of the machetes. Interesting. They seemed to want to keep him alive.

But stopping to attack seedy-looker had left one of the enforcers open to attack, and the fat guy with the ponytail leaped into the air with a surprising agility for one so large. Extending his leg as his momentum carried him forward, the fluid grace of the movement translated into a powerful kick that sent the enforcer sideways, his feet leaving the floor as his shoulder dislocated and the machete dropped from his grasp. He thudded into one of the tables occupied by a pair of businessmen, the flimsy wood collapsing beneath his weight.

He was out of the game, but his weapon wasn't. One of the drunk businessmen decided that this was just what he needed to spice up a middle-aged, boring existence and bent to pick up the machete, waving it around his head with a whoop of excitement. He began to charge toward the fighters.

Now here was one man who would surely get himself killed. Bolan sighed and raced to intercept him. Better this than having his neck broken or an artery severed by the other machete. In three strides, the soldier had caught up with the machete-wielding businessman and swung him by the shoulder with his right hand, the left balling into a fist that punched the surprised man under the jaw as his head swiveled. It was quick, clean and efficient. His lights went out, and the businessman dropped to the floor.

Meanwhile, the whip-thin triad hardman was engaging the other machete-wielding enforcer. The blade sliced through the air with grace and speed; it should have split the blond skull like a ripe melon. The triad hardman had more speed, more grace. He was under the blow before it had completed the arc, and his rigid fingers were driven toward the unprotected area beneath the ribs of his attacker. Despite being slowed and deflected by the flapping suit jacket and the lower end of the leather sheath for the machete, the blow still had more than enough force. The enforcer's eyes bulged, and air escaped from his open mouth with a gasp, followed by a hemorrhage of blood as the iron-hard fingers of his attacker splintered bone and pulped some of his internal organs. His friend had been luckier; at least he would live to fight again.

The fat triad ignored the man in the designer suit, who didn't seem to want to get his hands dirty, and hadn't entered the fray. Bending with an equally surprising suppleness, given his paunch, the triad hardman hefted Seedy-looker over his shoulder.

Bolan considered the triad men the threat. Maybe he could have a few words with one, if the two men were neutralized. The trouble was, no one in the club knew whose side Bolan was on, least of all the friend of the businessman he had just taken out of the game. The soldier had expected the customers to make a run for it, not to try to take him out. It was still noisy in the club, the music for the dancer blaring out regardless of the situation, no one bothering to turn it off. So

Bolan didn't hear the wild approach of the other fat businessman until the attacker was right on him. Hearing a yell and the last few approaching steps, the soldier whirled in time to see the chair the man held above his head begin to descend.

There wasn't enough time to get right out of the way, so the Executioner did the next-best thing. He thrust up an arm to take the brunt of the impact and dropped to the floor to take the momentum out of the blow. The chair was deflected with only a jarring blow to his elbow, then the businessman tumbled forward with a surprised and frightened look, his own momentum causing him to fall unexpectedly. Bolan hoped to complete the fall with a backward roll that would take him clear and bring him to his feet again. Unfortunately, the flailing legs of the falling businessman became entangled with the soldier's, leaving him unable to complete the maneuver. Twisting, he fell awkwardly, seeing some of the other customers headed for him.

They either saw him as an easy target, or some of the single table customers were part of the same mob, but he was now in big trouble. By the time he righted himself, they would be on him, and from all sides. From the corner of his eye, he saw the soundproofed door open, and the security man joined the fray, holding what looked like a hunting knife, which he pulled from a sheath on a leather thong around his neck. But he wasn't moving toward the Executioner—his prey was over near the bar, where Ponytail had Seedy-looker over his shoulder, and the peroxide whipcord was closing on the man in the designer suit.

And where the guy in the rumpled suit was finally detaching himself from the bar and approaching Ponytail. There was something about the way he was standing that suggested he had a lot of guts but not a lot of skill. He looked determined but scared. And if Bolan could see it, then you could bet Ponytail would have caught on instantly.

Another innocent bystander...although the three men advancing on the soldier as he finally kicked his leg free from the prone businessman and sprung back onto his feet were far from innocent. The second pair of businessmen had rushed past the security man when the door had opened, and these guys were obviously allied to the man in the designer suit in some way.

They formed a triangle around the Executioner, making it hard for him to keep them all in view. He circled, sensing their hesitancy as they kept out of his reach, hoping that it would make one of them stumble, make a mistake he could use to tip the balance his way.

It happened. The lean guy who had been sitting with a hooker, and who was grasping the beer bottle he had earlier been drinking from, took a step forward, waving the bottle. As his arm moved out, the soldier pivoted and kicked, catching the right side of the attacker's chest and throwing him back. He sprawled across a table, dropping the bottle and putting a hand to his cracked ribs. The gap his exit created gave the soldier space to adjust his position and face both the remaining attackers. They immediately rushed him, hoping to take him off balance.

They had severely underestimated him. Bolan was ready for them, an open hand taking one under the chin as he approached, the rock hard palm catching him with such force as to break his neck, snapping his head back and up. The second man tried to chop at the soldier as he approached, but Bolan blocked the blow with his forearm, swinging around his free hand to take the thug on the rib cage, breaking at least two of his ribs with the force of the blow. The thug folded, and as he did a loafer caught him full in the face, rendering him oblivious. Which left the bottle guy in need of mopping up, as he was starting to rise groggily from the broken table. Bolan turned and reached for him, taking him by his thinning hair to get his face in range before finishing him off with a blow that broke his jaw.

Without breaking sweat, the soldier turned to the remaining action. The peroxide triad hardman and the knife-wielding security man were circling each other, looking for an opening to attack. Both were too wary, and it looked to be a stalemate. But the guy in the rumpled suit was having problems with Ponytail. Even with Seedy-looker slung over his shoulder, the giant triad enforcer was unconcerned when the rangy stranger moved in to punch him in the gut. The blow seemed to make no impression beyond a grunted exhalation. Ponytail slung out a giant ham of a fist with his unencumbered hand that his curly haired opponent only just managed to dodge. He didn't fare as well from a follow-up kick that caught him on the knee and dropped him in agony. He tried to rise, but the nerves in his leg refused to obey, and he crumpled again. Ponytail gave a chilling smile, enjoying toying with his ill-matched opponent.

For whatever reason, Rumpled-suit had grit and determination, and Bolan was pretty sure that whatever side he was on, it wasn't one otherwise represented in the room. The Executioner picked up a broken table leg from where the first enforcer still lay unconscious and approached Ponytail from the rear. He whistled to alert the man, who turned to see the table leg being used as a club. Hampered by the burden on his shoulder, his attention was focused on blocking this attack, not noticing that Bolan's real point of entry was at groin level. As the club uselessly hit a brawny forearm, the soldier's loafer found a point in his opponent's groin, the searing, burning pain causing the man to lose balance and drop his burden. As the twin handicaps made him momentarily lose balance, Bolan closed on him, taking a bottle from the bar, where it lay miraculously unshattered. That state of affairs didn't last for long, and the sharp edge of the broken glass made an effective wound in the headman's neck, gouts of blood pumping with his heartbeat. His fingers sought to clamp the wound, but already they were becoming nerveless as the loss of blood caused him to black out. Unless he had immediate attention, he was a dead man—and there was no one to help.

Rumpled-suit was managing to stay upright while he stared at the dying Ponytail in disbelief. His expression told Bolan that the guy was out of his depth here, which left three people representing an immediate danger.

The peroxide whipcord and the security man were still engaged. The triad hardman flew at the security man, who waved the knife, not knowing where to aim. A flood of blows deadened his limbs, the knife falling uselessly to the floor as he lost balance. A sickening crack greeted the double blow that shattered the vertebrae at the base of his neck. The triad enforcer immediately spun to face Bolan, aware of what had happened to his colleague.

The Executioner assumed a balanced stance. Odds were that, despite his own expertise, his opponent was a better martial artist. But he couldn't watch his own back, and before he had a chance to make the first move, his eyes suddenly widened in surprise before glazing over as he dropped. Falling forward, he revealed the hunting knife buried in his back.

The man in the designer suit shrugged as Bolan looked at him.

"I don't know who you are, and I don't care. But now I owe you nothing, and you owe me nothing. Go, you'll get no other chance."

Bolan looked across at Rumpled-suit. "Get him," he ordered, indicating Seedy-looker, who was just coming around.

"No, he stays," the man in the designer suit snapped.

"He stays, I stay. I stay, you don't. Understand?" Bolan replied.

The man shrugged. "There'll be other times." His voice was heavily accented, and Bolan couldn't place the origin.

The Executioner motioned to the Rumpled-suit, who hefted up the recovering Seedy-looker. They backed to the soundproofed door, Bolan keeping a watchful eye on all angles.

Once out of the door, they hurried up the stairs. On the street, Seedy-looker was almost back to normal.

"What's—" he began.

"Shut it and be happy, Arnie," the Rumpled-suit interrupted him. "Just get into hiding before they come after you. You've had a lucky day—your luckiest."

"Yeah, but—"

"No buts, Arnie. The Maltese hate you, and now the Chinese'll want you dead, too. Just get out of town and keep lower than your usual sewers."

Arnie said nothing, but gave both of them a puzzled glance before backing to the nearest alley and hurrying away without a backward glance.

"As for you," Rumpled-suit said, turning to Bolan, "I don't know who the hell you are, but do I owe you big time or what?"

"You can pay me back by telling me what that was about, and how you fit in," the soldier replied.

"Yeah, yeah, sure. There are a couple of questions I'd like to ask you, but if we're going to get to know each other in any meaningful way, then we'd better not stick around here much longer if you know what I mean."

3

The streets of Soho were still thronged with tourists and thrill seekers, none of whom seemed to be aware of the battle that had raged in the cellar club. Despite this, Bolan's curly haired ally looked nervously around and then beckoned.

"Come on, let's get out of here."

Bolan said nothing, but followed the wiry man down a couple of side streets until he reached a battered sedan with a faked Doctor On Call sign in the windshield.

"Better than being towed away from a no-parking zone," he said when Bolan threw him a questioning look.

They entered the vehicle, and the ignition caught on the third attempt, causing the driver to sweat and curse. He maneuvered the ageing vehicle out into the main streets of Soho, casting quick, nervous glances to each side. Bolan sat low in his seat and scanned the area with a calmer eye. Maybe the driver knew whom he was looking for, but the soldier was pretty sure he'd be able to spot any trouble.

The battered sedan pulled out into Oxford Street, headed across Tottenham Court Road and then through Bloomsbury until they reached Euston Road. They headed toward the less tourist friendly environs of Islington and Shoreditch. It wasn't until they arrived at an area called the Angel—although there was nothing heavenly about the urban squalor as far as Bolan ironically noted—that the man in the rumpled suit seemed to relax.

"Thank God for that. I thought we wouldn't get out of there in one piece," he muttered, almost to himself.

"You wouldn't have," Bolan replied matter-of-factly. "It was both brave and stupid to take on a triad enforcer if you don't know what you're doing."

"I didn't, I'll admit," the driver interrupted.

Bolan nodded. "In which case, it may be a good idea if you told me why you felt the need."

The driver shrugged. "Call it a sense of civic duty, an obligation to my fellow man."

"Call it a lie," the Executioner snapped.

The driver eyed him with interest. "Yeah, well, apart from the fact that you're a much better fighter than me—which isn't saying much—you must have had more than an obligation to step in like you did."

Bolan mused on that; it cut both ways. True, he was following the triad enforcers to see what they were up to, but wasn't his whole mission, his purpose in life, an obligation he felt to even the odds for the innocent? How could he answer that in a few words?

"Okay," he said finally, "I'll cut you a deal. I'll tell you why I was in that club, and you tell me what you were doing there, why they didn't want to use guns and why you let Arnie run away. Well?"

The soldier's companion took a corner before answering. "Yeah, sounds all right to me." He shrugged.

So Bolan explained about the firefight at the airport, and how he had lost the trail of the Serbs before recognizing the triad enforcers, he had followed into the club. And when the fight cut loose, he felt obliged to deal with it, for the same reasons he had tried to intervene at the airport. He used the cover name of Mike Belasko, which was on his passport, explaining himself as a U.S. Justice Department employee on a fact-finding mission for his government.

The driver listened in silence until Bolan had finished his story, and even then didn't speak for some moments. Finally, without looking at the soldier, he began.

"I saw something about the massacre at Heathrow before I left to look for Arnie. And I've got to tell you, they've got you on video and on the footage that the TV stations are using. If you wanted to stay incognito, friend, you've really blown it out of the water. I'll say one thing for you, though— the cameras don't do you justice. I don't know if I would have recognized you if you hadn't told me about it.

"There's one thing, though. I recognized the Serbs, all right. And if I did, then you can bet your ass that the police have, as well—"

"What?" Bolan interrupted. "Those men are known to you?"

The driver nodded. "Oh yeah, and a couple of lovely little lads they are. Very good to their mothers...never go home," he added with a wry smile that came out as a bitter grimace. "There are a few people like them doing freelance work for local gangs. They've run from authorities in their homeland, and now they're picking up work wherever they can get it."

"Yeah, I've come across their kind before," Bolan noted.

"Exactly. I don't know what you've found, but the way I see it, the better they are, the better the mob they fall in with. These guys must be shit, because they're scraping the barrel with the Maltese."

Bolan frowned. Maltese? From his prior experience of London, he knew that the Maltese gangs that ran the vice rackets in Soho were allowed to run by the Mafia only on receipt of a cut from profits, a proxy way for the Italians to sew up the vice game in London with little fuss and violence. He said as much to the driver.

"Oh yeah, up until a few years back I would have said you were on the money," he said as he directed the vehicle toward the eastern stretches of the London suburbs. "But things went a bit pear shaped for the Mafia and the Maltese, didn't they? The *mafiya* started to spread its wings a bit, and the Yardies became a force to be reckoned with."

"Yardies?" Bolan queried.

"Jamaican-born gangsters who work London. Anyway, the Chinese figured they could get a piece of the action. It kind of worked like this—you know how organized the Russians are, right? Well, the Chinese didn't have enough of a population in the country to get manpower in and keep control. And although there were enough West Indians, the Yardies had never really had a central focus. They were always too laid-back and independent to be a threat in that way. But—and this is where it got nasty—the Russians coming in made the Yardies realize they had to get their act together in terms of organization. And with all these parties starting to put pressure on, then there was enough conflict of interest going down for the triads to put on a bit of pressure—"

"Which is why I saw some guys from San Francisco strolling through Soho like they own the town," Bolan interjected.

"Which they might if there's enough fighting going down. But anyway, you sound like you're familiar with organized crime over here."

"You could say that. It's been awhile, though."

The driver took his eyes off the road long enough to give Bolan a shrewd look before continuing. "Yeah..." he said slowly. "Anyway, in that case I'll assume you know about how it used to be. London divided up between two or three local gangs—the Krays, the Richardsons, the Maltese—with no influence to speak of outside the capital, just an understanding with gangs in other parts of the country."

"Quaint—a mom-and-pop business," Bolan murmured wryly.

"Right, what we'd call a cottage industry. Small in scale, but everyone having a vested interest in keeping the balance. Which is why it was always hard for outsiders like the Mafia and the triads to get a real foothold. But times change. Trouble is, the Maltese have had real difficulty getting up to speed with this change, and they've been hiring in muscle. But they're cheap bastards, and they've gone for the bottom end of the market. Which is why they get loose cannons like those Serb bastards."

Bolan acknowledged the information. "So the Maltese are hanging on to their share of the market, and using low-grade enforcers who are more a danger to the public and the Maltese themselves than they are to the other gangs."

"You got it." The driver nodded. "The police know those

faces, and it won't be long before they're putting pressure on the Maltese to give up the bastards, if only as some kind of sacrificial offering or appeasement."

"It wouldn't bother me at all if these guys wipe each other out. It makes life easier. But this could get really dirty."

"You call what happened at the airport today anything else?"

Bolan shook his head and said grimly, "No, but I've had the opportunity to see a whole lot worse. Someone needs to mete out justice for what happened today, and what could happen needs to be stopped right now."

"Listen, friend, you may be up to this sort of action, but you saw how bad I am at it...."

"You're no coward, but you're unskilled." Bolan shrugged. "I can handle this. There are ways you can help me without having to endanger yourself or anyone else by your lack of combat expertise."

"That makes me feel a whole lot better," the driver commented before adding, "I suppose I'd better tell you who I am, then, seeing as you've told me who you are. My name's Danny Sugarman." He extended a hand across the steering wheel for Bolan to shake. "I'm a private detective, and not of the Mike Hammer mold, if you know what I mean, hence being so useless when it comes to the violent stuff. I'm more your sort of divorce, serving-writs, looking-for-missing-dogs type."

"Then how did you get caught up in a gang war?"

Sugarman laughed. "If you grew up in the part of London I did, then the Krays and the Richardsons are like old Jewish folk tales—you can't escape them when you're a kid, even if you want to. Honest people love a bit of scandal about crime. Spices up their lives, and maybe makes them feel thankful it's not on their own doorstep."

"Which it is—and coming over the threshold if kids think it's an easy life."

"I don't know about that—I never did." Sugarman shrugged.

"You're a private eye—was there something glamorous that attracted you to the profession?" Bolan asked, casually making conversation.

Sugarman howled with laughter and thumped the steering wheel hard.

"Damn, if only you knew how funny..." he began, wiping tears from his eyes and negotiating another corner. Catching his breath, he continued, "Listen, Mike, it was nothing so much as a chain of mishaps that got me this far. I've screwed up every job I've ever tried, and the last one was a security guard for an investment company up in the city of London. High finance, safe deposit, all that. But it was night watch, when the magic eyes were on, the TV cameras in operation, time locks with no override on the safe doors...security tighter than a nun's—well, all the firms knew it. No one would try to knock it over at night. All I did was watch satellite and cable TV all night, and read more paperbacks than you've had hot meals. Safe job. Boring, even. But that was the problem, wasn't it? One of the alarms shorted one night, the key holder turned up with the police and yours truly was sleeping on the job with a porn channel on the TV instead of wide awake with eyes glued to the video monitors."

"Ah..." Bolan sighed. "So why choose something that you're not suited for and has any degree of danger."

"I didn't choose it, it chose me." Sugarman gave a wry grin as he noted Bolan's raised eyebrow. "No, it happened by accident. My wife had a colleague at work who thought his wife was fooling around. He knew I was a security guard, thought I was a hard man, and asked Steph if I'd do a bit of snooping. Next thing you know, I'm a private eye with an office, a semiregular income and a partner. And it's his fault that I'm out of my depth."

"How's that?" the Executioner queried. They seemed to be on the edges of the city now. The roads were less busy, and the streets were mostly residential, with more houses than apartment buildings. Stretches of parkland and green space marked it as a suburb. Sugarman pulled off the main drag and began to negotiate the back streets, slowing down and seeming more relaxed. Obviously he was close to home.

"Well, it's like this," he explained. "Justin's a good guy at heart, but when I met him he was a journalist caught up in some kind of fraud frame-up. I was looking for a missing kid, he was after some missing money and it all got a bit out of hand. He got fired, and sort of joined me without me actually having much say in the matter. He's got a bit of a temper, and kind of likes the adrenaline thing when a fight kicks off. Which is okay as long as he doesn't drag me into it."

"Which he did this time?"

"Got it in one, Mike. You see, Justin took on this job. A kid—a girl, only fifteen—called Samantha True, who'd run away from home. She'd been doing crack and had a boyfriend who was a dealer, and smoking too much of the profit. So much so that he'd got himself into debt and tried to do a disappearing act. But the suppliers—who just happened to be allied to the Maltese—had caught up with him. And he brokered a deal with them—they could have this nice piece of chicken—Samantha—if he was let off the debt. So she disappeared."

"What about the boyfriend?" Bolan asked coldly.

"Don't worry about him. We found out who was supplying him the hard way—for him. Like I say, Justin's got a temper on him, and he's got a sister the same age as the missing girl. I think that's half the reason he took the job. Let's just say that our little pusher friend won't be doing too much business after taking a fall off the top of a parking garage...in fact, he's permanently out of business."

Bolan nodded. "One less cannibal. But what about the girl?"

Sugarman pulled into a parking space and turned off the engine. "So far, the trail runs cold when you reach the man with the flashy suit. He's the big noise at the moment, and he's hard to get to. Which is where Arnie comes in."

"I was wondering when he'd make an appearance."

Sugarman's expression soured. "Yeah, Arnie's not the most savory of characters, but he's been useful, and he may be again. Which is why I felt obliged to save him and then let him go. He's low-life pond scum, but harmless compared to the people he works with—maybe 'worked' is more accurate, now. He's a greedy little bastard, and the money he was getting as a runner for the Maltese wasn't enough for him. So he'd sell information. To Justin and me, to the police and to the triads. He was easy meat for them, but they weren't too fussy if their sources of information became common knowledge. I guess that, from their point of view, it couldn't hurt to let the Maltese know that the reason they were being turned over was because their own people were betraying them. Which is why good old Uncle Arturo and his boys were asking Arnie a few questions."

"And why he expected them to come to his rescue. They 'owed' him," Bolan added dryly. "So who exactly is this Arturo?"

"Arturo Sartini, Maltese ganglord. Hard by their standards, but a pussycat next to the triads and the Yardies, as he's been finding out."

Bolan sat silently for a few moments, considering his position. Finally, he said, "I want the Serbs for what they did. I also have old business with the triads—the kind of business that's never settled. With the Serbs liable to take their fight to civilians, you can't rely on the scum to wipe itself out without bothering the innocent. I'll help you and this Justin try to find Samantha, if you'll help me."

"How, exactly?" Sugarman asked warily.

Bolan understood the man's apprehension. "It's okay, I won't expect you to fight when it's not your strength. But this is your territory, and you know the lie of the land. I'll need that intel if I'm to tidy this up as quickly and cleanly as I'd like. The other thing I'll need is some hardware, and I figure that if you don't know where to look, then this guy Justin certainly will."

"Check," Sugarman agreed. "It sounds like a good deal to me. I can't speak for Justin, but you can ask him in a moment. He'll be waiting for me."

They got out of the car and moved toward one of the terraced houses. The downstairs window was lighted, and two people were visible through the glass.

"Steph always waits up for me when Justin's around," Sugarman explained as they walked to the front door. "She's convinced he's going to get me killed."

"Will he?"

"Not if I can help it." Sugarman grinned as he put his key in the lock.

The Executioner stayed Sugarman with a hand before they entered. "What about Arnie? How long before he'll give up on you and Justin?"

"Soon as they get hold of him, the spineless bastard. But he's a good runner, and we've got a little time before they catch him—"

"We'll just have to move fast," Bolan finished.

He wouldn't have it any other way.

4

As they entered the lounge, the two figures visible from the front window rose to greet them.

"Dan, what the hell have you been doing?" a woman asked, the concern showing in her eyes as much as her tone as she hurried forward. "Your clothes—and those marks," she added, noting the rumpled and torn state of her husband's suit and the contusions on his face. Bolan hovered in the doorway, waiting for her to calm down.

The other occupant of the room, however, seemed impressed by Sugarman's state.

"Jeez, Danny, you've been laying it on a bit. I always knew you had it in you," he said, playfully punching Sugarman on the arm and grinning.

Bolan looked him up and down. He was maybe a few years younger than his partner, with a heavy build that was running to fat, even though he still looked powerful. His gut was beginning to spill over blue jeans that were ripped at the knee and faded, held up by a studded belt. An overhanging T-shirt advertising a heavy-metal band and a denim vest failed to hide his expanding girth. He had several days' growth of beard, and dark brown hair pulled back in a loose ponytail. But there was nothing so slack about the way his bright eyes flickered over the Executioner.

"Looks like you bought some company home with you, as well," he remarked, "and I'll be betting you came off better than our Danny, by the look of you," he added.

Bolan stepped forward. "You must be Justin," he said. "I'm Mike Belasko. Danny helped me get out of a bit of trouble. Nothing serious," he said diplomatically, as he noted Stephanie Sugarman's concerned expression. She was wearing glasses, which she pushed back up the bridge of her nose as she looked at Bolan.

"Yeah, Justin Stamp. Well, it's a pleasure to meet you, mate," Stamp said, holding out his hand, which Bolan took. The grip was firm, but brief. His eyes were still searching Bolan for clues.

Finding nothing, he directed his gaze to Sugarman. "So, did you get any sort of a result, Danny?"

Sugarman grimaced. "You could say that. There was a little bit of a fight."

"It's all your fault," Stephanie snapped at Stamp. "Before you came along—"

"Steph, don't," Sugarman said with some embarrassment, looking at Bolan. "This isn't the time, okay?"

His wife sighed. "If you say so. I suppose you're not going to talk about it in front of me?"

"What do you think?" Sugarman countered. "We'll go to the office. Won't be long, Steph, I promise."

"You always say that."

Bolan was glad to be out of the house and in the car before another word was said. Stamp was an unknown quantity, but Sugarman was undoubtedly out of his depth here, and with a wife who was that concerned, it would probably be best for him to be out of the business altogether. There were some jobs where it was impossible to sustain relationships. When you walked with death, your life was already spoken for.

"We'll go to the office, fill you in there," Sugarman said briefly to Stamp as they got into the car. The long-haired muscle man just nodded briefly, and they traveled the short distance in almost total silence.

"You never told me why they were only using knives tonight—no guns," Bolan asked of Sugarman.

"I'll answer that," Stamp said, turning in his seat to face Bolan. "There was a little accident a few weeks back, some of the merchandise got shot instead of the intended heavies."

Bolan gave the big man a puzzled look.

"Don't worry, it'll fall into place once we've completely briefed you. We're here now," Stamp added as Sugarman pulled in to the curb.

The office the two private detectives shared was above a shop on a small street, opposite a bar called the Red Lion. The last customers were still leaving when Sugarman turned the key on a glass-fronted door squeezed between a pharmacy and a fast-food chicken restaurant. They mounted a darkened and uncarpeted stairway until they came to a half-paneled door with D. Sugarman Investigations written simply on the door. The turn of another key, and they were in the office. Sugarman flipped on the lights and pulled down a blind. A red light winked four times on an answering machine, but Sugarman and Stamp ignored it. Stamp took a bottle of bourbon from a filing cabinet and placed it on the desk along with three mugs he took from a tray that also held a kettle, a bag of sugar and a jar of instant coffee. It was a sparse office, and as there were only two chairs, Bolan remained standing, allowing the two detectives to sit. Stamp gestured with the bottle and poured a measure of the spirit into all three mugs when the Executioner nodded.

"So, is either of you going to tell me all about it?" Stamp asked, screwing up his face as he took a sip of the warming bourbon.

Sugarman looked at Bolan, silently offering him the chance to begin. The Executioner shook his head, and Sugarman launched into a concise account of the evening's events from his own viewpoint. He added a few details about the case as explanation for Bolan, and his recollection of the fight was detailed. He was an excellent observer, and neither downplayed nor exaggerated his role in the proceedings.

"Sounds like fun," Stamp observed wryly when Sugarman finished. "So where do you fit into this, Mr. Belasko?" he added, turning to the Executioner.

Bolan explained about the firefight at the airport, and how he had arrived at the club.

"Yeah." Stamp nodded as Bolan finished. "It all kind of fits. I saw that shit on TV. You're lucky that the video didn't catch you full on—otherwise the police would be combing town for you like they are the Serbs," he said. "As it is, it's going to be hard to find those bastards, because Santini will have them hidden away."

"It doesn't matter how hard it is, I'm going to find them,"

Bolan said simply. "It seems that what I want jibes with what you want. We could be useful to each other. But I know combat situations and people who can handle it, and with all respect, Danny, I don't think that's you."

Sugarman held up his hands. "Hey, you don't have to tell me. We've already talked about this."

"I just wanted to clear that up for Justin. As for you," he continued, turning to Sugarman's partner, "I have no idea what you're like in combat situations. Danny says you can handle yourself. Can you? And remember, you're putting me and yourself in danger if you lie or exaggerate."

Stamp bit his lip for a second before replying. "You know," he said slowly, "that could easily be taken as quite insulting, but you're a pretty straight down the line guy, so I'll be the same. I can handle myself in a fight, and I know a bit about guns. But by the standards of these guys, and particularly by yours, I'm a beginner. I don't know what I'd be like in something like the Heathrow firefight—a bit of roughing up criminals, maybe handling a shooter if it comes my way...that's my level."

Bolan considered this. "I'll be frank with you, Justin. You're overweight and haven't been in the forces or in organized combat activity. But you seem to be levelheaded, and you've got guts. And by all accounts you're not found lacking when you have to take the big leap and wipe out the scum...because if we don't, then they'll take us out. It's that simple. Do you understand?"

Stamp nodded. "Yeah. It's clear."

"Then we make a plan of action. I have the background to this from Danny, but I'll need specifics. And I'll need weapons. Do you know where I can get weapons?" he asked Stamp.

"Oh yeah, I know a little. But it's just a few lowlifes who sell stolen revolvers, and I reckon you'll want something a bit more powerful than that."

"I'll want an SMG, maybe a semiautomatic rifle of some kind. Handguns—revolvers and automatics. A hunting knife, something like a Tekna or maybe a Wilkinson Sword. And I'll need some grenades if you can get them. Frags for sure, maybe some gas."

Stamp whistled. "You set your sights pretty high, Mr. Belasko. Higher stakes than I can offer." He shrugged. "That's way, way out of my league, or the guys I know. Now, they may know someone, but the problem with that—"

"Is that it makes ripples that turn into waves. And not the kind of waves we want," the Executioner finished.

"I can help," Sugarman said softly.

Stamp looked at his partner with a puzzled frown. "You? This is a side of yourself that you've been hiding, Danny, my man. You're not having me on, are you?"

Sugarman shook his head slowly, and from his solemn expression, the Executioner knew that his problem had been solved. His instinct that Sugarman was an intel man had held up.

"Well, don't hold out now," Stamp said quietly, echoing Bolan's thoughts. "What's it all about?"

"Benny," Sugarman said, shrugging.

Stamp screwed his face up in disbelief. "Benny the informer? That's ridiculous! He..." And then his face lit up as realization dawned. "Shit, I get it—he gets the blind eye because he's an informant, and everyone except those really in the know think he's a snide petty thief with a big mouth."

"Exactly." Sugarman nodded. "Except I don't think even the police realize the extent of it. I only know because of

Frank Gaunt. He was a cop I knew who got killed a couple of years back," Sugarman explained to Bolan. "He told me about it because of this weird thing that went on a few years back over where he worked, in Docklands and Mile End. There was a bunch of rogue cops took the law into their own hands, going up against the Mafia and the triads, and taking out the Yardies before they'd really got their act together."

"It's understandable, as long as you make sure no one innocent gets hurt," Bolan commented. "After all, that's what we're going to do."

"Yeah, but they weren't so careful. And two cops Frank knew got onto them. They were nearly killed, but they managed to take out a lot on both sides. They disappeared after it happened, and there were rumors about the spook squad signing them up, but I don't know...what I do know is that they got themselves tooled up by Benny. And they had some major-league hardware, the sort of stuff you're after. And I wouldn't mind betting he's still in business."

"Sounds like our man," Bolan said. "We should go."

"Too right," Stamp agreed, rising to his feet. He turned to Sugarman, who had remained seated. "So, you coming or what, Danny?"

Sugarman shook his head. "Belasko's right. I'm more of a liability for this. You go—and tell him I told you about Frank and the fuckup on Wanstead Flats a few years back. He'll know that you really know, then, and aren't just sniffing around."

"What are you going to do?" Stamp asked.

"I'm going back to Steph and try to calm her down," Sugarman said. He tossed a set of keys at Stamp. "You take the car, I'll walk. I'm not out of this totally, but Belasko's right again. I'm better at the backroom stuff. I'll handle that end of it."

"It's the right call, Danny," Bolan said, "and don't think that I think less of you for it. The opposite, in fact." When Sugarman had acknowledged this, Bolan turned to Stamp.

"Okay, we need to move fast. You can brief me on anything more on the way."

WHEN THE CAR WAS WINDING through the back streets of East London, moving in from the suburbs to more built-up, run-down areas, Bolan told Stamp once again exactly what he had learned from Sugarman, and the background the man had given him on the case they were handling.

Stamp chewed on his lower lip as he took a corner, a habit that Bolan had already noticed as evidence of deep thought on the big man's part. Finally, he spoke.

"The background to how the Maltese and the Chinese have been operating in the past is sound enough, but the further we've gotten into this case, the more it looks like the two parties—partly at the instigation of Artruro himself—have been trying to build some bridges and make some alliances. The Maltese pimp is sick of being small-time, and he knows that his people have been pretty insular in the past. Something the triads are definitely not. Old Uncle Artie has ambitions for his girls, and he likes to get them spirited out of the country for a bit of the old white slavery. A nicely turned white ankle is highly prized in territories where there aren't a lot of them. Weird, really, because I've always thought Indian girls were the prettiest in the world, but there's no accounting for taste. Accounting only talks in pounds sterling and U.S. dollars, right? And while he's at it, Uncle Artie's getting his girls to do a bit of drug courier work, as well. Mules for the triads, sold through their slavery rings, and a nice profit for the man from Malta. Meanwhile, in a nice little switchback, it turns out that the Maltese are acting as a front for laundering some of the money the triads are bringing in through these activities. Heads they win, tails they win—like a crooked casino. Not a bad little gig if you can get it, I suppose."

"If you like misery, pain, degradation and suffering. And don't have a conscience," Bolan said softly.

"Exactly, Mr. Belasko. I knew I liked the way you thought," Stamp said with an equally firm gentleness. "See, the police are either taking bribes, or are hamstrung by those who are, with a consequent lack of evidence and a failure to get the bastards put away. So the Chinese and the Maltese carry on with impunity. The only fly in the ointment is the fact that they don't really trust each other. The Maltese are fly bastards, and the triads want to take them over in the long haul. Honour among thieves? Don't make me laugh. Some bleedin' comedian made that one up. So it's an uneasy alliance at the best of times. That's what I meant about a little accident earlier. A delivery got screwed up because some of the muscle got trigger-happy with each other and took out some of the girls while they were at it. You don't waste good merchandise like that, which is why they've got this agreement for blades not bullets...kind of a peace-making plan. But it's real knife-edge, if you'll pardon the bad joke. It's waiting to blow up big time, and I reckon that if we can get this going, we can actually pull back a little and watch them do the work for us."

"As long as it brings the Serbs out into the open. There are a few scores that need to be settled with them, by people who can't. So I just want to lend a little assistance," Bolan said.

Stamp chuckled. "That sounds fair to me."

"What about the girl?" Bolan asked after a pause. "If we can avoid endangering her in any way, so you can get her out..."

Stamp sighed, and there was a sadness in his voice when he spoke. "Poor little Samantha, getting involved with scum like that. Cracked out of her brain, laid by anyone who had the price of a few rocks, then used to settle a debt. We've been trying to find out where she is—is she in the country, has she already been shipped out?—but we just keep drawing blanks. I haven't said, and I know Danny hasn't, because he knows her mum and dad from way back, which is why we took it on. You're not supposed to know that, by the way. There are no other secrets, but that's just between you and me, and that's why he's taking this one to heart. I reckon she's dead. Either through an OD, so something related to her habits, or just because she made trouble or was a liability. See, there's a chain, and we've uncovered some of it, but she leaves the loop before we reach the end of what we've found. So I reckon she's long since gone—" he paused, before adding softly "—and I hope it's a better place, you know?"

Bolan assented grimly. Now he had the full background, he understood why the two men were prepared to take greater risks than they had before. Sometimes even men who have their own self-imposed limits were driven to actions beyond their normal boundaries. Which was why Danny Sugarman had been at the lap-dancing club, and why Justin Stamp was prepared to delve into armament in a bigger way than ever before.

The Executioner spoke a chilling finality. "It seems to me that we both have scores to settle for the innocent."

"Yeah," Stamp agreed, "amen to that."

He pulled up in front of a house that was tucked away

off Roman Road, the main street market for the Bow area of the East End. There was new money in the area, old slums being renovated, but this house still had a dingy, dangerous air. The paintwork seemed to have grime trapped in it, and the front door showed scars of being forcibly entered in the past.

"I'd take a rough guess that we've arrived," Bolan commented wryly.

"Whatever tells you that?" Stamp chuckled, shutting off the engine.

The two men left the car, and Stamp knocked on the door. They waited a few moments, Bolan noticing the high-tech surveillance camera almost, but not quite, concealed in the wooden door frame. And he'd bet that the wood concealed a steel frame set in concrete. This house wasn't as vulnerable as the occupant would want visitors to believe. Eventually, they heard the sounds of footsteps approaching the door and several locks being turned. The door opened to reveal a grinning West Indian, around five-five, with a large gut hanging over the elastic waistband of his jogging pants and a cigarette hanging from his unshaved jowls. He grinned broadly, nodding his head at both men, the woollen hat keeping his dreadlocks in place moving in time.

"Mr. Stamp! This isn't like you, making social calls on my humble abode."

"Nah, Benny, talking to the police is more your style, isn't it?" Stamp replied.

Bolan was amused to see the little man's expression tighten, his eyes go cold. But his tone remained mock friendly. "Why, Mr. Stamp, you'll get poor old Benny in trouble, making accusations like that."

"It's nothing compared to what I'll say about your real line of business, and in a loud voice, if you keep us standing out here."

Benny stepped back and ushered them in, closing the door behind them and catching all the locks.

"Ras claat," he swore under his breath, "should've known Babylon has no waiting."

"Leave me out with the Rasta lark, Benny," Justin said with a sigh, "it's as fake as the rest of your cover. I remember you when you were a kid actor from Leyton, getting on TV and in the local papers all the time. You've been good at hiding all your life. But this is serious. We've got big money, and we want to do some serious business."

Benny cocked his head to one side, squinting at them. "Whaddaya mean?" he asked in broad cockney, the Rasta patois and the stoned demeanour suddenly dropping.

"Danny said to remind you about Wanstead Flats—Frank Gaunt told him before he kicked it."

"Aw, fuck, I always knew that would come back to haunt me," Benny said. "I thought once Frank was gone... Shit, Dan's kept quiet about that for a few years."

"Emergencies only, Benny," Stamp said quietly. "We're not big shooters, but we need some serious business right now. Mr. Belasko here knows weapons, so don't try to rip us off, or you won't get out of the house in one piece."

Benny eyed Bolan suspiciously. "What sort of man comes to my house to trade and makes veiled threats?" he asked.

Bolan returned the stare with a graveyard coldness. "A man who would normally stop your trade, but who has need of it to prevent more innocent death. You have my word that you'll be untouched. Believe me, if I just wanted the weapons regardless, you'd already be dead."

Benny looked away uneasily, having seen the steel in the

soldier's eyes. "You know what, I believe you," he said simply. "If you've got the cash, then let's do business and you leave before you run out of patience, man."

"You get the idea," Bolan assented.

"This way." Benny pushed past them and led them to a cupboard under the narrow staircase. He opened the door and flicked a light switch. The narrow cupboard triangulated with the dip of the staircase, and there was barely enough room for even Benny to stand upright. He moved an empty packing case, then a piece of tattered carpet to reveal a trapdoor set flush to the floor. It was carefully stained to match the surrounding old boards, and it was only the trained eye of the Executioner that allowed him to make out the boundary lines.

Benny ran his stubby, nail-bitten fingers along the edge of the trapdoor, and caught the concealed catch. The trapdoor swung open easily on well-oiled hinges to reveal a concrete stairway that led into the cellar.

"I didn't know these places had cellars," Stamp commented as they followed Benny down.

"They don't," the West Indian replied with a chuckle. "I got the idea from something I saw on the news a few years back. There was this old guy in Hackney who'd excavated under his house and made a load of tunnels that led under his neighbors' houses. He even had hidden exits coming out into their gardens. And he was smart—he knew how to avoid undermining the foundations on all the adjoining houses. They only found him because his own house caught fire while he was down in the tunnels. They couldn't find a body, but they wondered why he had electric cables running off his main supply and down under the manholes in the back garden. He was down there and didn't even know his house had burned down." Benny laughed louder.

"So you figured that would make a good armory," Bolan stated.

"Got it in one," Benny replied. "Took a bit of time to work out how to do it, get hold of plans and stuff and then to get it dug in secret, but it's worked out all right in the end."

"Except for the people who live above if your little arms dump goes off," Bolan said.

Benny turned. "That isn't gonna happen."

Bolan shrugged; they all said that.

As they walked through a section of shored-up tunnel, Bolan and Stamp had to bow their heads to cope with the low ceiling, although the shorter Benny was able to stay upright. After a few yards, they came to a room that was barred by a steel door hung off a concrete post.

"Figure we must be about two doors down now, Benny," Stamp commented. "Don't the neighbors ever notice any noise?"

Benny shook his head as he unlocked the steel door. "Deaf old couple, and I installed the post and door—and some soundproofing—when they were away. It's all planning, Mr. Stamp." He smiled.

Stamp and Bolan made no reply, but it was difficult for the soldier to restrain a whistle as the door opened out and Benny led them into his armory.

"See anything you want?" Benny asked with pride.

The room was the same height as the corridor and widened to about fourteen feet across. It was an equal depth, forming a square that was packed floor to ceiling with weapons, boxed and unboxed. The stacks were broken only by paths that ran between them. Bolan recognized the stenciling on some of the crates: there were M-60s with boxes of 7.62 mm ammunition; a cache of SWA-12 assault shotguns; boxes of Walther P-38s and Berettas with 9 mm ammunition; Israeli-made Desert Eagles and Uzis; Colt Pythons and Smith & Wesson M-4000 shotguns; assorted boxes of plastic explosive, and fragmentation grenades; and a clutch of old Eastern bloc weaponry including AK-74s and the later AKSU assault rifle with a shorter barrel and a folding stock, RGD-5 antipersonnel grenades, and CZ-75 semiautomatic pistols.

Benny had enough hardware stashed under his neighbors' houses to keep a small war on the boil for some time.

"How the fuck did you get all this stuff, Benny?" Stamp asked.

Benny shrugged, lighting his cigarette once more. "Just a knack, Mr. Stamp, just a knack. See anything you like?" he continued, unable to hide the pride in his voice.

"Desert Eagle, Beretta, SWA-12...and plenty of spare clips," Bolan snapped.

"Easy, easy, man—no need to be so rude," Benny said softly, busying himself collecting the hardware, which he then laid on top of a crate near the soldier. All the weapons were unloaded. Bolan reached for the Desert Eagle.

"Easy, easy," Benny repeated, holding up a hand. With his free hand he reached behind him and pulled an Uzi from on top of another crate. Bolan could see that this one was ready-loaded. Benny clicked it to short bursts. He smiled as he did so. "Don't think that it's anything personal, but I'd be really fuckin' stupid to let you load up down here when I had nothing."

Bolan merely nodded, but didn't stop from lifting and inspecting the Desert Eagle before sliding a magazine home and chambering a shell.

"And I'd be equally stupid to let you hold that on me

without being armed myself," he said calmly, leveling it at Benny.

Stamp laughed nervously. "Yeah, right, guys. And I don't actually have anything at all right now, so pardon me if I'm the one getting a little jumpy around here. I think I have more right than you two. Yeah?"

"Just get some hardware, Justin," Bolan said calmly. "I don't think Benny will mind too much as long as it's paid for."

"So where's the money, then?" the Rasta asked, unable to keep the tremor out of his voice.

"I'm going to reach into my inside jacket pocket very slowly and take out a wallet," Bolan declared. "Don't get jumpy."

"How do I know you ain't got a gun in there?" Benny asked.

"For God's sake, Benny, why are we here?" Stamp countered.

"To get more," Benny snapped back.

"It's a reasonable point," Bolan said calmly. "That's why I'm going slowly, Benny. Just watch..."

Stamp stopped gathering his own weapons—a Walther P-38 and a Smith & Wesson M-4000 shotgun, along with spare ammo—to watch what was about to transpire. Bolan reached very slowly into his jacket and withdrew the wallet, all the time keeping his eyes leveled on Benny. The Rasta's eyes were fixed on Bolan's hand as it reached for the money, and his relief was almost palpable when a wallet emerged in the soldier's hand. Bolan flicked it open, and Benny's eyes widened at the wad of high-note currency inside.

"Enough there to cover everything, Benny?" Bolan asked. "I'll have to count it, of course, and add up what you've bought, but I figure it should be about okay," Benny said, lowering the Uzi and stepping forward to take the wallet from Bolan's hand.

"Oh, Benny," Bolan said suddenly, as though remembering something, "you know what I was saying about leaving you untouched because there was a greater menace at stake? That was before I realized how you'd made your armory, and how much you had here. You're dangerous, and I think your business needs to be shut down." Before Benny could react, the Executioner smashed the butt of the Desert Eagle against the Rasta's temple. As the man collapsed to the ground, Bolan grabbed a set of plastic riot cuffs from a nearby box and tied Benny's hands behind his back.

"What did you do that for?" Stamp asked.

"Because this place is too much of a risk to those who live in the street above. Have you got any idea what would happen if it suddenly went up? I couldn't let that happen."

"So what do we do now?"

"You tell me," Bolan said briskly. "Call it a tactical exercise. Test your wits."

Stamp didn't have to think too long or hard about it. "For a start, we leave Benny down here for now," he began. "We load up with as much hardware as we can carry—and you give me a crash course in how it all works—then we move. In case we need to regroup and get more armament, we take the keys, and leave everything open bar the front door. That way we can let the police know anonymously about this cache when we're done."

"Sounds about right. We can let Danny tell the police, as he'll still be around."

"I wouldn't bet on it," the big man said, shaking his head. "I've known Danny a long time, and he's no fighter...but this one means a lot to him, and I know what's gone down between us, which you don't. If it comes to it, he'll get tooled up and come in with us. He's got more mettle than you think, and he won't be found wanting."

"I don't doubt that, but I don't want him to get that involved. He has other people to think of. I'm guessing that you don't, like me."

The big man nodded. "Not anymore. But you still shouldn't underestimate Danny."

"Okay. But before anything else, we need to get fully equipped, and I need to brief you."

They spent the next half hour in gathering together a good sample of the equipment that Benny had collected for sale. As they unwrapped each handgun, rifle, shotgun or grenade, Bolan showed Stamp how to fit the ammo, prime the grenades, and how to fire with them to avoid the whiplash effects of the different recoils. He talked smoothly and rapidly, making the big man repeat the lesson twice, as soon as he had finished. Then, once he had been through every item, he called items at random, making Stamp go through a weapons drill. It was an almost surreal situation, but it was necessary. If they were to use any of these weapons in the heat of combat, then it was necessary that the big man was immediately comfortable and familiar with them. A moment's hesitation could cost either—or both—their lives.

At last, they were ready. Stamp was a quick learner, and as the drill progressed, Bolan was sure that the big guy wouldn't be found wanting when it came to a firefight. Satisfied, he loaded up, wishing that he had a blacksuit or combat vest to comfortably house the weapons. As it was, they would be hard to conceal, and difficult to store and withdraw effectively.

"We'll load the car, and just keep a minimum on our person at this stage," Bolan said decisively. Stamp agreed, and the two men ferried the armament up to the ground floor of the house, then out into the trunk of the car, working in relay to keep a watch on the vehicle. When the trunk was locked and loaded, they returned to the cellar in order to secrete the personal armament they had previously chosen.

With a last check that the riot cuffs were holding, they left the house, Bolan triggering the locks externally from the infrared on the key chain he had taken from the Rasta. Then he paused, looking up at the concealed camera. "Damn," he muttered. "Just a sec," he said over his shoulder, then entered the house.

He made a quick recon of all the rooms, looking for security monitors. He guessed that if Benny had the outside wired, then the rest of the house—and particularly the cellar—had to be similarly set up. He found the monitors in Benny's bedroom. There were six of them, corresponding to six cameras, and they were all wired up to video recorders. He took the tapes from all six, as he and Stamp would be on most, if not all.

He hurried out of the house and slipped into the passenger seat of the car. "Something we wouldn't want anyone to find," he commented briefly. Stamp nodded, not bothering to ask further questions, and slipped the vehicle into gear.

When they hit the main road into the West End of London, Bolan asked where they were headed first.

"A nice little club that'll still be open," Stamp said, checking his watch. "It's a raver's paradise, with chill-out rooms and an Internet café. Part of the slavery ring is tied into the operation of the cyber café, but I'm not sure how."

"The chances of trouble?" Bolan asked.

"Strong," Stamp replied. "It's run by the Chinese, and they'll be pissed about earlier tonight. My guess is that Uncle Artie will have put the blame firmly on your shoulders, showing them an edited version of the security camera video. So you'll have your card marked."

"As long as it's in the open, that's all right with me," he said quietly.

5

The city streets were relatively quiet until they reached Soho. Only the lines of people waiting for night buses to take them out to the different areas of London from the corner of Tottenham Court Road and Oxford Circus showed that there was any nightlife at all. Bolan couldn't help but contrast this with any other major city in Europe or the U.S.A., where all-night transport kept the city alive 24-7.

Soho, however, was another matter entirely. Cabs, motorbikes, drunken revellers and drugged-out party animals drifted across the roads regardless of oncoming traffic: hedonism was rife in at least one quarter of London.

The one thing that did concern him was the greater police presence on the streets, some of the officers discreetly armed. Although he hadn't seen any TV news, it was a good bet that such an outrage as that at the airport had brought out a larger police presence. And that the chase between himself and the Serbs had been noted. It would have been a very stupid police force not to find the scratched BMW in Soho and connect it to the fight in the lap-dancing club. Police intel would tell them that the Maltese had Serb heavies on their payroll.

He would have to tread very carefully.

Bolan checked his watch as Stamp maneuvered the car through the crush and found a side street that was relatively quiet where they could leave the vehicle. It was just past 3:00 a.m., not yet twelve hours since the Serbs had terrorized Heathrow.

Stamp cut the engine and they got out of the car. The big man looked at Bolan questioningly.

"What about...?" he said casually, indicating the trunk of the car with a movement of his head.

"No, not right now," the soldier replied. "We've got no way of concealing any of them, and the area is crawling with police. They'll know the Serbs got as far as here, and they'll know about the fight earlier."

Stamp nodded. "Yeah, they're not that dumb. So what do we do?"

"How much of a danger is this club?" Bolan asked.

Stamp chewed his lip for a moment. "We'll need to get what we're carrying past the doormen, and they're bound to search us. But after that, mostly blissed-out ravers, kids with no desire to fight. It's only the staff heavies we need to watch for."

Bolan assented. "I don't want innocent kids to be in danger. Will we have to fight our way past the doormen?"

Stamp cracked a vulpine grin. "Ah, now, that may not be necessary. Hang on a moment."

The big man walked around and opened the passenger door of the car, reaching into the glove compartment. He grimaced as he rummaged through the detritus collected within. "I'm always telling Danny he should clean his bleedin' car once in a while. God knows what he's got in here— Ah, hang on...."

He triumphantly flourished two laminated passes. Each had a photograph in the corner, but the faces were obscured by tags pushed through each to secure them to a string. Stamp pushed one over his head and handed the other to Bolan.

"Local council environmental health authorization. With these, we can just walk in and they wouldn't dare search us. Last thing they want is bring attention to themselves by roughing up a representative of the body that grants them their license."

Bolan looped the pass over his neck. "Nice touch," he said, holding the tag. "I take it you or Danny borrowed these?"

"Could say that." Stamp smiled. "We've used them a couple of times, but never at this club. So we haven't been checked out by these guys, and we've had no problems so far."

"Let's hope your luck holds," Bolan commented.

Stamp locked the car and walked out onto Dean Street, one of the main roads running through Soho. Bolan followed at his shoulder.

"It's just round the corner, literally," Stamp said briefly as they walked less than two hundred yards before turning off the main drag and onto another side road.

Two large heavies in black polo shirts and pants stood out from the colourful and mostly skinny crowd that was gathered around a blue neo-Georgian house.

"Spot the security," Stamp murmured as they approached. "Leave the talking to me—just flash the pass at them."

Bolan followed Stamp through the crowd around the door, ignoring the affronted cries of those who had been lining up for some time to get in and resented what they saw as line jumping. It did occur to the soldier that, although he was in a suit, Stamp may perhaps look too casual—no, make that just plain untidy—for a health-and-safety inspector.

"Hello, lads. Local council, routine check on the sanitary facilities and the kitchen. Won't keep you long," Stamp said with a weary air as he approached the doormen, holding up his pass. Bolan could see they were wearing headsets, and he scanned the frontage for any security cameras.

The two heavies exchanged glances.

"Oh, come on, lads," Stamp said quickly, "this is the tenth place we've done tonight, and we've still got another four before we can go home. My wife hates me doing nights." He sighed heavily.

It worked. The doormen looked amused and waved both Stamp and Bolan through.

"You want me to tell the manager you're here?" one of the heavies asked.

Bolan's hand flexed, ready to fight, but Stamp headed the threat off at the pass. With a raised eyebrow, he said, "This is supposed to be a surprise visit, isn't it? Come on, Mike, let's get this done and get on to the next one," he said to Bolan, leading the way in.

The soldier followed, acknowledging the friendly nod of the doormen with one of his own. So far, so good.

Once they were in the club, Bolan followed Stamp as the big man led him through a maze of corridors, past rooms where dancers raved to pumping techno, past chill-out rooms where music and ambient sounds like whale song lulled exhausted clubbers, and past other rooms where darkness and light shows competed for attention with differing strains of dance music. It was a world the Executioner saw very little of, and it was a world alien to him. They also passed the washroom facilities for the club. At the bar area, soft drinks and "energy" drinks were sold at vastly inflated prices along with the bottled water that seemed to be the staple of the clubbers. It didn't take much to work out that Ecstasy and MDMA powder had replaced alcohol in this club.

Bolan moved closer to Stamp and said in his ear, "There'll be security cameras. We should at least make a show of checking the facilities you mentioned."

The big man shook his head. "Soon as we were in here, those goons on the door would've been on their headsets to the manager, and he'll know that there isn't a visit from the locals scheduled. That's all sorted with bribes, so they can get around the licensing conditions. So we need to get what we need and get the hell out."

Bolan nodded and followed the big man up a flight of stairs, past several exhausted and tranced-out clubbers who were sweatily recovering away from the dance rooms. Turning left, they entered a room where the thumping of a repetitive beat was only a distant memory. And it was quiet, which enabled the two men to talk with greater ease.

The room was lined with tables that contained computer terminals. There was also a hexagonal arrangement of terminals in the center of the room, utilizing as much of the space as possible. Not that this was necessary, as only a few of the tables were occupied at present, with a few desultory singles and couples surfing the net.

"So tell me why we've come here to do this?" Bolan

asked as Stamp went straight to one of the terminals and logged on, tapping in the address he wanted.

"Because this club is a link in the chain that leads from little Samantha to the Far East and a bunch of assholes in white slavery. And the site I'm calling up is their own Web site. We know that it's used to convey messages to the contacts overseas, and that it's part of the machinery they use to transport the drugs and the girls. I want you to look at it, and to look at it here, so that we're in the right place to kick some ass."

Bolan scanned the room and caught the security camera. "And you've figured out, of course, that as soon as they catch on to the fact we're phony, they'll be using the security cameras to track us."

"And they'll see us screwing around on the Net. Yeah, if that doesn't bring them running..."

Bolan grinned mirthlessly. "That'll certainly shake them up." He leaned over Stamp's shoulder. "What do we have here?" he murmured, studying the Web site the big man had called up.

At first glance, it seemed innocuous. The site extolled the virtues of the club as a "multidimensional" dance experience, and had links to other clubs and also to record labels specializing in the music. There seemed to be nothing there that could offer a clue. But then the Executioner hit the links for other sites related to rave culture outside of Britain, and found links to the holiday island of Ibiza and the Balearics, islands where there was a strong all-year-party ethos relevant to clubbers. There were personal and club sites, but only one site that related to a travel business. Bolan thought rapidly, knowing they were on borrowed time in the club: links from this site should lead to agencies where clubbers could book holidays in these islands, but instead there was only a single link—and this wasn't to an agency that covered these islands. Instead, the A-rave-daze agency specialized in holidays that hit the hippie trail to India via Indonesia.

"Where does the chain run out?" the Executioner asked Stamp.

"Well, well, what a coincidence," the big man said, taking a look over Bolan's shoulder. "Would you believe that it happens to be Indonesia, just by chance?"

"Running a legitimate business ferrying youngsters to the East, and using some of them as mules while they're heading to slavery. A good cover. We need to find out where this company has its offices," he added, noting that there was only an e-mail address, no indication of an office address or phone number. Prospective customers could only contact the company electronically, which was very convenient.

"No problem. A quick call during office hours to a friend of mine should sort that. They'll still be registered somewhere, even if they try to keep everything in cyberspace. It's just knowing the right place to ask."

"Good," Bolan said, "because I think we're about to get some incoming."

As he had been hurriedly reading through the on-line material, searching for clues, the soldier had also kept his senses alert for any changes outside the Internet café room. The club was well soundproofed in order to separate the sound systems in the different rooms, but it was impossible to block out all sound. And as the ambient level of sound within the café was low, it was possible to hear noise on the staircase outside. Bolan was soon able to pick out several men— maybe five, six pairs of feet—clattering up and down the stairwell to his level.

"They're coming from above and below, to pincer us. So we'll have to try and take them out from both directions at once. What's the layout at the top of this building?"

"Stairs to the roof, then a fire escape down the back."

"They'll have that covered. What about the roof?"

"All these terraces of old buildings have walkways across them for repairs and maintenance, so we can get from one end of the terrace to the other."

Stamp tried to turn to face the doorway, but Bolan restrained him with a hand, his face still directed toward the terminal.

"No, don't look around. They'll have headsets, and you can bet we'll be watched from the security camera. Try to look like we're unaware, but be ready to turn, hit the deck and fire when I say. We'll play it as it comes. I'd rather chance the roof than have to fight our way down and out onto the street. Too many unarmed people around."

"What about them?" Stamp asked, with a nod of his head to the other occupants of the room.

"Enough cover if they're quick, and I don't plan on being in here long," Bolan replied. Then, as his senses told him that the security guards were on them, he shouted, "Go!"

The two men turned and hit the floor, rolling apart to widen the necessary angle of enemy fire. Stamp took the Walther P-38 from the waistband at the small of his back, bringing it level in a two-handed grip. Bolan went for maximum firepower, unlimbering both the Desert Eagle and the Beretta.

The first of the security men had reached the door. Two of them charged in with an Uzi and an MP-5. Their headsets had told them that the enemy was unaware, and the sudden screeching in their ears as they were told otherwise was ren-

dered superfluous as the P-38 cracked twice, taking out the
Uzi toter with two holes to the chest, while a tap on the
Beretta danced a four-hole line up the body of the surviving
gunner.

They weren't English or Serb heavies—they were Chinese. So the club had to be another uneasy alliance between
the Maltese mob and the triads.

The other occupants of the Internet café were thrown into
terrified confusion, some diving for the scant cover offered
by the tables, others trying foolishly to head for the exit—
through which more security men were charging.

Four innocent clubbers were cut to ribbons by bursts of
Uzi and MP-5 fire as they ran into triads who fired on sight,
not caring whom they hit. Screams of pain, deafening blasts
of fire and showers of blood and tattered clothing filled the
doorway, making it hard for Bolan to tell what was happening. One thing he could be sure of was that his wish to leave
the club without innocent bystanders being hurt had already
been blown away; another was that the triads weren't dressed
in black like the doormen. They looked like ordinary clubbers, which would make them hard to pinpoint in the gloomy
lighting.

"Go!" Bolan yelled to Stamp as he rose to his feet, the big
man following. "Cover the left," the Executioner ordered,
moving over the bodies and firing on the run. The triad gunners behind the falling ravers were momentarily unable to
target their quarry, and bursts of fire from Bolan and Stamp
took them out of the play.

The doorway was now empty, a bizarre stillness settling
as the two men reached the open portal. They flattened themselves against the wall on each side.

"On three," Bolan said quietly, before counting them in.

They both fired around the doorjamb before risking a look. The right—Bolan's side—was leading down. The stairwell ended in a landing that had a club room off to one side with the angle to the next flight of stairs obscured. The left led up, and Stamp could see that it was empty as far as the next landing. But there was no club room up above, only the administrative offices.

The two men pulled back into the room.

"We're on three," Bolan snapped. "How many more?"

"One floor, then the roof," Stamp replied curtly. "But that's where the private quarters are."

"So maybe better security and a lot more triad guns," Bolan finished. "Down is going to be hard, but at least we know the lay of the land."

"How do we do it?"

"I'll go first, you cover the back. Keep it real frosty, Justin, and we'll do this."

"Count on it. I'm too young and pretty to die yet," Stamp countered with grim humor.

"Let's do it," Bolan snapped, moving into action.

The two men left the room, hugging the near wall to make themselves a difficult target from the angles below. Bolan took the stairs two at a time, Stamp following with his P-38 directed upward. A burst of MP-5 fire from above ripped chunks of plaster from the wall above their heads. Stamp cut loose with two rounds, driving the attackers back to cover.

Now Bolan was at the angle of the stairwell. Bizarrely, the noise level in the dance rooms was such that people were still dancing in the room off the landing, oblivious to the gun battle going on outside.

At least it would keep them out of harm's way, Bolan thought, scanning to see if there were any armed occupants.

There wasn't. It seemed that the triad gunners wished to keep the battle contained on the stairs. The soldier deduced, therefore, that there were no exits on any of the dance rooms other than the doorways leading onto the stairs. It probably broke every fire regulation in the book, and—more importantly right now—it also meant that the soldier was faced with no options but to keep going down.

"Position behind?" he demanded.

"Clear," the big man affirmed.

"On three, covering fire to next landing, move in relay."

At three, Stamp stepped out and laid down covering fire as Bolan moved down across the landing and down the next flight of stairs, keeping low and firing sparingly with the Beretta. There were three triad gunmen positioned in the stairwell, two of whom were immediately immobilized by fire that took them in the head and chest. Bolan then flattened himself against the stairwell wall and laid down cover for Stamp to move down, the big man reloading the P-38 as he descended.

They took stock of their situation on the landing, the club room opposite still pulsing to a relentless beat. Bolan hoped it would stay that way, and the clubbers would keep out of the line of fire. He looked at Stamp, who was red-faced and breathing heavily.

The big man caught the look and grinned. "Not used to this sort of excitement, Mike. Just out of shape...but keep on, I'll manage."

"Okay, we repeat the maneuver. One floor left." Bolan reloaded the Beretta and Desert Eagle with full clips as he spoke. They would be necessary before they got out the front doors of the club.

"Let's do it," Stamp replied.

Without pause, they repeated the tactic that had got them down the last flight. This time they were greeted by no opposition. Two reasons: first, the enemy wasn't going to repeat the same mistakes; second, they were now on the ground floor, the stairwell opening onto a downstairs club room and an enlarged hallway, where the cash booth was positioned.

A cash booth that represented a strong, secure position for the triads hardforce, while the corridor leading past the stairwell gave an ambush point from the rear.

Bolan took the lead as they stole down the stairs, keeping low. "Cover the rear," he directed, raising both his guns and pouring fire into the booth. It had an opening through which the two gunmen could fire while keeping almost totally covered. So he concentrated his fire at the narrow gap, hoping to at least prevent the gunmen from firing. The sustained fire drew better results: the Parabellum and Magnum slugs pouring into the booth wiped out the gunners inside, covering the interior with a spray of blood.

Stamp was running backward, unloading on the fly as the enemy gunners presented targets. He couldn't dodge their return fire, and prayed that his luck held.

So far, so good.

As Bolan and Stamp headed toward the exit, a few ravers near the entrance of the techno room, perhaps hearing the chatter of gunfire above the thumping rhythms, walked into the lobby of the club and came face-to-face with two men wielding guns and a cash booth that was a bloody mess.

The two women and three men screamed in shock and terror, then hastily turned back toward the safety of the dance floor.

Outside, there were more screams of fright and harsh shouts in a language Bolan could identify as Mandarin—

more gunmen were closing off their avenue of exit. The two security guys in black appeared in the doorway, each holding a Walther P-38. Two taps on the Beretta and the gunners were drilled from groin to neck as they raised their weapons.

"Incoming," Bolan yelled. "Too many people out front, no idea of how many armed."

"They're moving up the back, as well," Stamp affirmed, firing off a couple of shots and hitting one gunman. But one wasn't enough. "C'mon," he said, grabbing Bolan and pulling him toward the club room.

"Too many people!" the soldier growled.

"No choice," Stamp retorted.

Bolan's gut tightened at the thought of the possible massacre, but he had little choice but to follow, as Stamp had already raced into the room. The music stopped suddenly, and the panicked murmur of the crowd was almost palpable.

It gave the Executioner a chance to cut the risks to the innocent in there. As he followed Stamp, he fired a burst of rounds into the ceiling, yelling, "Move to the back!" in the silence that followed. The cowed and terrified crowd responded to the stimulus of fire, as the soldier hoped it would, and began to move backward. Simultaneously, Bolan pushed Stamp to one side of the doorway and flattened himself against the wall.

There was no way out of the room. A crowd of innocent people huddled against the far wall, and an unknown number of gunmen headed their way from two different directions.

Bolan had gotten out of far worse situations. His primary concern now was to prevent loss of innocent life, which meant going in hard and swift. That was their only hope.

"Just follow me," he yelled at Stamp. The big man, his

eyes registering the seriousness of the situation, merely nodded agreement.

The footsteps just outside the door, now only too audible in the relative silence. Bolan judged his moment, then stuck the Beretta around the doorjamb and stroked the trigger twice. Gurgling screams and the sounds of bodies hitting the floor told him the shots had been effective. He whirled and began firing with both guns, keeping himself partially concealed by the doorjamb while picking off targets. On the other side, Stamp was also partially concealed, his revealed hand pumping shots from the P-38 with less rapidity, but going for accuracy.

The triad hardmen were in confusion, turning to flee from the hail of death but instead running into the path of their cohorts' gunfire. Those who survived fled mostly out of the open front doors, with some retreating down the back corridor.

"Move—grab some hardware," Bolan shouted at Stamp, keeping the Beretta in hand but holstering the Desert Eagle to leave a hand free to gather a brace of MP-5s as he moved over the carnage he had created. There were ten or twelve dead Chinese in the hall of the club, and he had to leap over the corpses as they obstructed a clear run to the exit. The big man followed, scooping an Uzi and an MP-5 on the run, training the P-38 on the rear exit.

They made the street with no further attack. Bolan rapidly scanned in both directions, but the side street was empty, clubbers having fled in panic, the triad gunmen having also disappeared.

"No one's behind us," Stamp reported as he joined the soldier in the street.

"We need to get back to the car and get the hell out of here. Listen..."

Wailing sirens approached from the east—at least three cars by the sound of it.

"This way," Stamp said, heading toward the end of the street that emerged into Wardour Street, where they had left the car.

He wasn't going to get that far; a phalanx of Chinese and some Maltese hired muscle rounded the corner and took up defensive positions in the basement stairways of the old houses and behind parked cars. They cut loose with their subguns, sustained bursts that forced Bolan and the detective into cover. Stamp yelled in surprise, skidding to a halt and managing to throw himself sideways behind a car that found its paintwork irretrievably damaged by the volley of gunfire his presence attracted. He immediately slung the MP-5 and brought up the Uzi to return fire.

Bolan took cover behind a railed basement area and laid down a covering fire with one of the MP-5s he had taken. Hearing the blast from behind him, Stamp took the opportunity to break cover and head back toward the Executioner, keeping low and zigzagging, as he had seen in movies. He had never felt more out of his depth, but knew somehow that if he could just keep upright, his companion could get them out of there. Some of the fire had been diverted toward the Executioner, which gave Stamp more of a chance. He dived into a basement recess and came up with his Uzi firing.

Despite the heat of the situation, Bolan was still impressed at how the big man had quickly grasped basic tactics, and as Stamp laid down suppressing and covering fire, the soldier was out of the basement area and down the road to the next stretch of cover. As soon as he gained it and began firing, the big man was out from cover and moving back.

So far, there was little sign of the opposing forces having

covered the other end of the street. Could they have been that sloppy, or was there a reason why they were holding back?

"Where does that lead?" he asked Stamp.

"Poland Street—right away from the car," the big man replied.

"Why are there no Chinese from there?"

"It'd take them a long time to get around there from Wardour, and it's too busy for them to hang around."

"Okay, let's get there quick, before they have a chance," Bolan shouted to the big man. "Now go!"

Stamp broke cover and headed for the end of the street as Bolan laid down covering fire. He knew it would be hard to come out into a main thoroughfare and then lay down fire for his companion's last retreat, but then again he also knew he was taking a risk not checking the road in each direction before skidding out and around the corner.

Despite the noise of gunfire from the side street, the occupants of Poland Street seemed to be carrying on as though nothing untoward was happening a few hundred yards away. Stamp got only a few curious glances from passersby as he tore out onto the sidewalk with an MP-5 on his back, a P-38 stuffed in his belt and an Uzi in his hands. Hoping that no one would interfere, and that no triad hardmen were approaching, he braced himself at the corner of the street and laid down fire for Bolan to make good his full retreat. He tried to ignore the sirens, which were growing closer by the second.

When the soldier emerged, he immediately headed to his right. His sense of direction, and what he remembered of the district, told him that this would bring them into Oxford Street, a more open expanse of road with less potential for surprise attack, and not as packed with innocent bystanders.

Stamp gave one last burst of fire down the sidestreet, then set off after the soldier.

Bolan cast an eye over his shoulder as he ran, to check that Stamp was following. The big man was red faced and short of breath, but adrenaline and a strong desire to stay alive had insured that he could keep pace. The two armed men had left a trail of confused passersby in their wake. The Executioner could also see some of the triad gunners and the hired Maltese muscle venturing out into Poland Street.

"Where...where...are we going?" Stamp panted, gasping to catch his breath.

"Out into the open, draw the bastards away from a crowded area. Can we get to the car?" Bolan replied, adding his own question as the sound of sirens zeroed in on them. Stamp shook his head, not risking the breath to speak.

The big man was tiring fast, and the sirens were catching up, as was the opposition. They would have to find a way of clearing the area, to draw the fight away from the crowd.

They ran onto Oxford Street, which at that early hour of the morning wasn't the busy thoroughfare it was by day or night. There was very little traffic, and they were able to dodge it with ease, as would the opposition gunmen pursuing them.

Stamp was tired of running. He knew he wouldn't be able to go much farther, so he decided to take matters into his own hands. He turned and faced an oncoming car, leveling his Uzi at the windshield before lifting it and firing a burst over the vehicle's roof.

Bolan stopped and turned at the sound. "What the hell are you doing?" he demanded. He would be damned if he would let Stamp do anything to endanger passersby.

"Can't run...only way," the big man gasped. Now holding

the Uzi with the barrel directed to the sky, he moved around the car, a powerful Peugeot sedan with four young men staring nervously from the interior. "Out now," he snapped. "Please," he added as an afterthought.

Bolan joined him, also keeping his Beretta and MP-5 directed upward, one eye on the triad hardmen, who were visible from the junction of Poland and Oxford Streets. They were closing, and would be in firing range soon.

"Please, get out of the car," Bolan said briskly. "You won't be harmed, but I can't speak for them," he added, gesturing down Poland Street.

The four young men, awestruck to actually see real guns stumbled out of their vehicle, leaving the engine running.

"Sorry about this," the Executioner said as he and Stamp climbed into the vehicle. "Now get the hell out of here. They won't be as reasonable as us."

As if to emphasize his point, the chasing Chinese and hired thugs began to open fire, wild bursts from out of accurate range lighting up the night air. Like a spell being broken, the four car-jacked young men yelled, scattering from the oncoming onslaught.

"Get us into gear and get us out of here," Bolan said to Stamp.

The big man responded by grinding the gears and revving the engine, tires squealing on the road as the vehicle picked up speed and headed toward Tottenham Court Road. The rear window starred and then dissolved into a shower of glass as the gunmen hit the main drag and fired at the retreating vehicle.

"Should be okay now," Stamp hissed, still struggling to regain his breath. "You sure know how to show a fellow a good time," he added, choking on his own laughter.

"It's not over yet," Bolan said grimly. "They've got head-sets, and they'll have reported us taking the car. And we've got to hope we can get past the incoming law enforcement."

"Uh, we've got pursuit," Stamp muttered, glancing in the rearview mirror. "Take a look."

Bolan turned and looked back. Behind them, three vehi-cles had skidded out of the side streets of Soho onto Oxford Street, screeching to a halt to allow the following gang of Chinese and mercenaries to scramble into the vehicles.

"Dammit, that's just the thing I want to avoid," Bolan cursed. "I don't want us to be driving through the city shoot-ing at each other. It's too dangerous, and it's too damn con-spicuous."

"So what do we do?" Stamp asked. "You want us to maybe take the fight out somewhere where it's open ground, and there's no one else around?"

"Yeah, because they're not going to leave it, and I think we should teach them a few simple manners."

Stamp smiled slowly and chuckled. "If they want a fight out in the open, then they can have one. I've got an idea where we can go. The only thing is, will this vehicle outrun them?"

"If it doesn't, then we're just going to have to stand and fight in the city, and hope the police don't catch up with us before we have a chance to dispose of this scum and make an escape."

Stamp looked in the rearview mirror and touched the ac-celerator as the Peugeot roared down Euston Road, on the route that Bolan had taken with Sugarman just a few hours earlier.

The Peugeot gained a little ground on the pursuing vehi-cles. They were struggling to keep distance, let alone gain.

"Oh yeah, I reckon we can keep them away until we want," the big man said. "Only thing I've got to do now is avoid the traffic cops until we get there. Keep our asses covered, Mike, and hold on. This may get a little bumpy."

6

The roads were almost deserted, and Stamp took the opportunity to put the pedal to the metal and drive the Peugeot to the limit of its capabilities—he had to if they were to stay one step ahead of the police and the enemy gunners. It was a necessity.

Bolan rode shotgun, making sure that the pursuing vehicles didn't get too close, but by the same token that they were able to keep the Peugeot in view: he wanted to take these guys out, but only when it was open ground.

Some of the route he recognized from earlier, but Stamp was keen to use back roads and twisting routes, pulling off the main roads as soon as possible.

"Where are we headed?" Bolan asked as they circled around a fenced-in green space off Bow Road, then heading toward Docklands.

"Nice little patch of open ground out near where Danny and I come from," the big man replied tightly, his concentration focused on the road. "Know it really well, and know all the cover."

Bolan smiled without humor. "Think we can recon the land before they arrive without leaving them too far behind?"

"I can brief you as we get there, Mike. Meanwhile, take a little look at this—it's the stomping ground of organized crime these days," Stamp said as they headed away from the East End and into the heart of Docklands. Bolan recalled that it used to be closed-down docks and slums. Now it was shiny, high-tech office buildings, the winking needle of the Canary Wharf tower like a beacon in the night, beckoning them closer.

Stamp continued, as he took them on a tight circuit of the empty roads. "Most of these businesses here are legit, but it's a good hiding place for organized crime to launder money and people. It might be the business center of London now, but it's also the sleaziest place in town."

"And good for leading these guys on a chase," Bolan added.

Stamp laughed, skidded on a turn and doubled back to take the road off of the self-contained island.

"Home stretch, Mike. Hold on."

Bolan looked behind and watched the vehicles with the gangsters struggle to keep pace. Stamp tapped the brake until they were closer and then maintained his pace, heading back toward the suburbs of East London.

They were taking a hell of a risk, staying on the roads so long. Once the police had arrived at the club and viewed the destruction, they would presumably link it to the atrocities at the airport—the fact that the Serb's BMW had been dumped in Soho, and had to have been discovered by now, would make for a link too strong to be crudely dismissed. Having made this link, it wouldn't take them long to find out about the convoy of cars barreling through the center of town.

Bolan knew that the city and West End areas of London were under heavy security as they had long been a terrorist target. Surveillance cameras watched all the main roads, ostensibly for traffic control and driving offences, but also to keep tabs on any unusual activity.

A string of vehicles roaring along the city streets came under the heading of "unusual activity" in the Executioner's book; he was sure the metropolitan police would feel the same. And if so, they would be using police choppers to track the convoy.

And yet, as he scanned the skies, he couldn't see a single aircraft. He knew that they had some black helicopters, as well as the standard white-painted traffic choppers, but even these would make some impression in the strong ambient light of the city.

Maybe they were just lucky; maybe Stamp's route had been so twisting and bizarre that the police couldn't get a handle on them.

The big man gunned the vehicle and headed for a bridge, taking it at such speed that the Peugeot took off as it reached the pinnacle of the incline, tires eating air for a few feet until it crashed down, the wheels spinning as they searched for a grip on the pavement. Stamp and Bolan were flung around the interior of the vehicle, the big man wrestling with the wheel.

"Shit, I won't do that again," Stamp roared, righting the vehicle and taking it onto a turnoff that brought them out into a residential area. They took a sharp right and headed over a railway bridge, past two apartment buildings...and suddenly it was dark. The street lighting disappeared, and the headlights of the following vehicles blazed brighter.

"Okay, listen up," Stamp stated. "That's the London Cemetery on the right. On the left is what's called the flats. It's just grass, no scrub or cover. We're taking a left and pulling onto it by a small lake. There's an island with only one sandbar leading onto it. The island has trees and bushes for cover. That's where we're going."

Bolan listened intently, taking in every word and analyzing the situation. It was a good ambush for the opposition as they tried to follow, but could also be a cage, keeping himself and Stamp trapped. But maybe the guys following wouldn't know the area like Stamp, and would figure there were more exits. It was so dark, even in the approach to dawn, that it would be hard for them to recon without taking time and leaving themselves open to attack—for, as Stamp had said, Bolan could now see the flat emptiness of the surrounding grasslands.

Stamp pulled off the road and bumped over the curb and makeshift sidewalk, skidding to a halt on the soft, marshy grass. Before the engine had died, both men were out of the vehicle. Stamp led the way, the Executioner following and keeping his eyes on the oncoming vehicles. Their headlights stabbed into the darkness, but didn't penetrate enough to illuminate the two men as they gained the high ground.

"Follow right behind—water's up, but only ankle deep," Stamp whispered hoarsely as he splashed into the shallows of the lake. Following, Bolan felt his loafers fill with water, and the soft surface of the sandbar sucked at his ankles. He let the suction claim his shoes, hoping that he wouldn't snag any tree roots while his ankles were unprotected and vulnerable.

Stamp crashed into the foliage on the island, stumbling and falling to one side, panting heavily. Bolan pitched to the ground, rolling and coming up to face the direction in which they had come. He checked the MP-5 he carried and found it nearly empty. He switched SMGs, his vision adjusting to the gloom. Scanning the area, he could see the outlines of the trees and shrubs on the island. It had a center that was empty, a round patch of turf and a fringe of dense vegetation all around.

Although there was no other way onto the island, if they allowed the Chinese and the Maltese to circle them, they could be caught in a cross fire. They would be hard to spot, but it would also be hard for them to fire through the dense wall of green. They couldn't let the enemy spread out. It was a good bet that the first instinct of the enemy would be to follow their path, so they had to try to keep them clustered by their vehicles and take them out quickly.

He spoke rapidly, outlining the ideas to Stamp, who had also switched to the MP-5 he had grabbed in Soho. The Executioner had barely enough time to rough out the battle plan before the enemy was upon them.

The two men separated and put some distance between them as the enemy vehicles screeched to a halt. It would make them a divided target, harder to hit, and would give them a greater arc of fire, something necessary to their tactics. They shouldered their weapons, ready to take action.

On the flats, the cars screeched to a halt, Chinese and Maltese gunmen spilling out before the vehicles had even ceased moving. There were shouted orders and imprecations in Mandarin and English, and some of the gunmen, wielding SMGs, began to run toward the island.

"Now!" Bolan yelled, tapping the MP-5 and sending a hail of fire into the first of the advancing groups. Some of the slugs cleared the gunmen and took out the lights on two of the cars, plunging the area into gloom. But most of the fire hit home. The four gunners in the lead were wiped out as the slugs traced bloody trails across their torsos, filling the air with a fine mist of blood as the smell of spent blood and emptying bowels drifted across the night.

The remainder fell back behind the open doors of the vehicles, taking wild shots in the direction they thought the fire had originated. There was still enough illumination for Bolan to be able to count those still standing. A total of nine opponents remained to be taken out. They had some shelter, but would have to move out from cover in order to try to attack. The thing was to stop them spreading out: keep them contained and within easy reach.

On Bolan's far side, two of the Maltese gunmen tried to move out in a wide arc. Stamp tapped the trigger of his MP-5 and dropped one of the gunners, the SMG fire tracing a line through his middle as he moved, almost severing the top half of his body from the bottom. The second mercenary caught a shot in the arm that spun him as he tried to scramble back to cover. He hit the earth screaming in pain as his torn arm gushed crimson onto the turf.

As this occurred, a trio of Chinese gunners tried to make a break from Bolan's area of fire, seeking to leave a gap between each runner, but not enough to make the first man out a sitting target. At the best of times, it would have been a difficult piece of timing, and against a soldier like Bolan it was tantamount to requesting execution.

The soldier wasn't one to turn down such a request. With the total calm that comes of being in command of your weapon and the situation, Bolan took them out one at a time with controlled taps on the MP-5. The first fell to a brace of slugs in the chest area; the second caught a burst that ripped up his rib cage, tearing apart his vital organs; and the third, suddenly frozen on seeing what had happened to the men just in front of him, half turned to fire but was nowhere near fast enough. A tracery of fire stitched him from groin to head, his torso and face reduced to shredded flesh and splintered bone.

By Bolan's reckoning that made four down, five to go. The odds were rapidly evening. The only problem was that the five were now sheltered behind the doors of one vehicle, penned-in on each side by the arc of fire from Bolan and Stamp. That made them hard to access, and time was at a premium. They needed to finish the job, then get the hell out before the police finally caught up with the action.

Bolan could really have done with one of those RGD-5 antipersonnel grenades that they'd found at Benny's. The trouble was, the ones they'd carried out with them were still in the trunk of Sugarman's car, somewhere in Soho.

"We've got them pinned," Stamp whispered hoarsely across the bushes, echoing Bolan's thoughts, "but we need to finish them."

"I know," Bolan said quietly. "Time to mix it up. Stay in cover and keep them there. I'll flush them out."

Stamp grunted his assent, and emphasized this by a quick burst of SMG fire to pin back one of the Chinese who tried to crawl out from cover. There was some return fire, but nothing to bother either man.

Time for Bolan to take the initiative. Keeping low, he ran to the back of the island, plunged through the foliage and stripped off his suit jacket before he started to wade into the lake. He knew he would make some noise, but there was little option. A few feet in, he looked around. He set off to his left, toward the closest bank. He kept the MP-5 above his head, and as soon as he felt the bottom of the lake drop away, he cast off, making broad strokes for the shore.

The first glimmerings of morning were beginning to lighten the horizon, and he cursed. The very thing that had been a boon was now a major problem—the lack of cover. He reached shore, then ran in a crouch until he had rounded the curve of the bank, and the enemy vehicles came into view. There was sporadic fire both from the Chinese and from Stamp, but they were at stalemate. Bolan hit the turf, flattening himself.

He was in firing range, but they would be able to locate him easily on the flat ground once he began firing. He'd have to hope that Stamp could back him up by taking out those on the far side of the vehicle when they moved.

In the growing illumination of the morning, Bolan sighted the enemy. Three stood on his side of the vehicle, with two on the blind side—and one of those may be out of action because of his injury. He had one chance to get the shot. The three were clustered close together because of the small area of cover, so they represented one large target instead of three small ones.

He tapped the MP-5, spraying a burst into the group. Instinct made them turn at the sound, but they were unable to return fire as the hail of SMG fire tore into their chests, blowing them backward. The three gunners were dead by the time they hit the ground.

The sudden attack had a galvanizing effect on the two men left in cover on the far side of the vehicle. They broke away from the car, separating and heading for the island, firing wildly. They had to have realized that there was only one man left on the island, and hoped to make a suicidal run to at least claim his life. The two gunmen, both Maltese hired guns, were making ground, but one was the man Stamp had earlier injured, and his gait was stumbling and erratic, as was his pattern of fire. His left arm hung uselessly by his side, and he had lost a lot of blood. He didn't get far before the big man picked him off with a burst of fire that left little remaining of his chest cavity.

But the second gunman kept running. The gunfire from the island seemed to have dried up, and Bolan felt a tightening of his gut. Instinct told him that Stamp was down.

The soldier rose into a crouch and began to zigzag toward the mercenary, who was still pouring fire onto the island. He was almost at the water's edge when Bolan sighted him with the MP-5, spraying a small arc of fire that caught the gunman in midstride, ripping into him. He stumbled and fell headfirst into the lake, his SMG falling into the water beside him.

Bolan kept running, heading for the sandbank path. He kept alert for any signs of life among the enemy, but they had all been terminated. The question was, had Stamp survived?

The soldier splashed across the gap between the flats and the island.

"Justin, it's Mike. Where are you?" he called.

The big man didn't reply immediately, but as he turned toward the area where he had last sighted him, Bolan heard a groan. In the early light of dawn he could see Stamp sprawled on the turf, pitched backward by a hit. The soldier came up beside the big man and dropped onto one knee. Stamp grimaced as he saw Bolan, trying to grin through the pain.

"It's not gonna kill me—I hope—but I didn't realize how much it'd hurt," he croaked.

Bolan studied the big man's wound. A lucky shot had ripped a chunk of flesh and muscle out of the top of his arm, near the shoulder joint. There was a lot of blood, but luckily the artery had been missed. Stamp was weakened and needed a doctor, but it could have been a whole lot worse. The soldier ripped off his shirt and used it to bind the wound temporarily. Then he started to help the big man struggle to his feet.

"I know it hurts, but we've got to move," he said firmly. "We don't have long to get the hell out of here. I can drive, but you've got to stay awake long enough to direct me."

Stamp tried to laugh, but it turned into a painful, hacking cough. "I figure I've got enough adrenaline pumping around my body to keep me awake for a month." He groaned as he leaned on Bolan for support.

The two men moved over the water and past the wrecks of the enemy vehicles. The one at the rear still had the keys in the ignition. Bolan bundled Stamp into the passenger seat and got behind the wheel, gunning the engine.

"Are your prints on file?" he asked suddenly, remembering that the big man would have left them all over the vehicle they had hijacked. Bolan would be safe. He didn't officially exist anymore, but if the authorities could trace Stamp, then everything would be blown.

"You know, the funniest thing is that I've never actually been arrested...yet," Stamp wheezed. "There's always a first time."

"Not if I move now," Bolan told him, turning the vehicle

and heading back onto the road. "Now, quickly, which way?" he added, hearing the sound of distant sirens.

It was a sound that had seemed to haunt him since arriving in London.

7

Bolan made the distance between the flats and Sugarman's house in next to no time. It wasn't too far, and having to provide directions stopped Stamp from fading away, which was the thing the Executioner wanted to prevent. He could hear police choppers in the night air, and hoped they weren't looking for him. With a bit of luck, there was so much carnage at the site of the firefight that, by the time the police had worked out that there was one car missing, and it wasn't the vehicle originally hijacked, he could ditch this vehicle somewhere safe.

It was almost fully light by the time he pulled up in front of Sugarman's house. Lights were still on inside, proof that the detective had been unable to sleep, despite his opting out of the action.

Bolan got Stamp out of the passenger seat and hoisted him

up, carrying the semiconscious man over his shoulder. The big man was right—he really was out of condition, and too heavy to be taking part in combat situations. But there was no doubting his heart or spirit. Bolan found the deadweight hard to balance for a second, then jogged the short distance to the front door, which was already opening, revealing a startled Sugarman.

"Justin? Is—"

"He's alive, but not for long unless we get a doctor. Nothing vital's been hit, but he's losing blood. Do you know someone who will treat a gunshot wound in confidence?"

Sugarman nodded, reaching for the phone. Like Bolan, he had realized that there was no way that Stamp could be taken to a hospital or an everyday physician. Although Sugarman hadn't been party to the firefight, it was obvious from the condition of his friend, and the blood and filth that covered the Executioner, that something pretty spectacular had occurred.

Sugarman barked into the phone, "Tyler? It's Danny... I don't care what time it is, I've got a serious problem. It's Justin—he's been shot.... I don't know, do I? I just know he can't go to the hospital. He's losing blood, so unless you want your little secret to get a bit more known... No, son, it's a promise, not a threat.... Good."

Danny slammed down the phone. "It's cool—we've got a lot on him, and he does know his business. He'll be about five minutes. He's near here, and he'll hurry. What happened?"

"I'll tell you later. First, let me put him down, and then I've got to get rid of the car we arrived with."

"Let me do that," Sugarman said. "I know places around here where it won't be seen for days. Besides, you look kind of conspicuous."

Bolan looked down at himself. It was a good point.

"Bring him through here," Sugarman continued, leading the soldier into the den. The couch was long and wide, enough for the big man. There was no way for Bolan to let him down gently, and Stamp groaned and recovered consciousness as he hit the cushions.

"Sorry," Bolan whispered. "There's a doctor on the way."

"Good," Stamp whispered through gritted teeth. "I need a good dose of painkiller right now."

Bolan heard the front door close and looked around. Sugarman was gone. The engine of the stolen car fired into life, and the soldier heard it pull away.

He also heard the door to the den open, and a gasp of horror. When he looked around, he saw Sugarman's wife standing on the threshold. She was wearing a toweling robe, which she clutched around herself in shock and horror when she saw Stamp on the couch.

"What happened to him?" she asked, coming across to examine the wounded man.

"He stopped a bullet. It looks worse than it is, fortunately," Bolan told her. "Mostly a flesh wound, some muscle. Blood loss is the big problem. If he needs a transfusion, then there are going to be some awkward questions asked."

Stephanie Sugarman shook her head. "Not if Tyler's coming," she said softly. "He makes my flesh creep, but there's no one better if you're in deep and need to hide it."

"Sounds like an interesting man," Bolan said wryly.

Stephanie looked at him with eyes flashing anger. "I don't think it's very funny."

"Neither do I," Bolan replied levelly, "but getting uptight isn't going to help. Justin's alive, and it sounds like he's in the best hands. I didn't ask him to get involved, or your husband. Just the opposite, in fact."

Her expression softened. "I know. Danny told me when he got back here. It's just that I didn't expect... Where is Danny?" she asked suddenly, realizing that her husband had disappeared. Bolan explained briefly.

"You'd better get yourself cleaned up, Mr. Belasko. There's hot water, and you should see if something of Danny's fits. That suit's just about had it, and looks a bit suspicious if you go out in daylight." She looked the soldier up and down. "You're roughly the same height, and I'd guess you're about the same measurements. You're broader, so the shirts and waists may be a bit tight, but I think you should find something. I'll look after Justin until Tyler gets here."

Bolan readily agreed, and as he left the room he heard her talking to Justin, asking him what the hell he and her husband had got themselves into. It didn't ease his conscience any as he took a shower, the mud and grime washing away more easily than his worries.

He just couldn't get a handle on this. It seemed like a standard mob operation, but why had the Serbs gone ballistic at the airport? Was it because of the bubbling gang war tension, or was there something he was missing? What had they been expecting to pick up?

The fact that he felt guilt over Sugarman and Stamp didn't help. They had offered their services freely, but the crucial difference was that he was a trained soldier, an expert in combat. They weren't; far from it. They were in over their heads, and they were good men, with a sense of honor. One of them had a wife to consider, and the other was bleeding all over the carpet right now. It shouldn't have been this way, and he felt responsible.

Such thoughts would help no one. Bolan filed them away in the back of his mind as he dried himself, then selected a shirt and a pair of blue jeans from Sugarman's wardrobe. They were inconspicuous enough for now. He hoped they were the same shoe size; otherwise he would have to send someone out to shop for him in the morning.

He caught the light coming through the drapes. It was morning already.

When he had finished dressing, he went back down to the den. Sugarman was back, and he was standing in front of the couch. A short, immensely fat man was leaning over Stamp, his breathing more heavy and labored than that of his patient. A stand was feeding a blood bag into the big man's arm, and his wounds were dressed. The fat man looked around as he heard Bolan enter.

"Ah, you must be the mystery man responsible for waking up half of East London this morning. The radio was full of it when I was on my way over. And I haven't seen so many police since the last IRA bombing campaign in the docks. You've certainly created quite a stir for just the one of you."

"How is he?" Bolan asked, ignoring the man's tone and asking the only relevant question.

"He'll live." The medic shrugged. "From what I hear, you must be used to this sort of injury, as it was a most accurate analysis. Now that it's stitched and bandaged, he should be fine. He'll need more blood, but I've left another bag in Danny's fridge. And he's on enough painkillers to keep a junkie happy for a month. But other than that..." He shrugged again. "Time is the great healer, as with all things."

Tyler spent a few more minutes fussing over Stamp, then gave Stephanie instructions on the blood bag and the painkillers, and left. Bolan sat the Sugarmans down while

Stamp rested, and in detail outlined what had happened during the previous night. They listened in silence until he had finished, then Danny spoke.

"So what about my car?"

The soldier nodded in understanding. "If they're searching vehicles left in the Soho area, then we've got a problem—a real one. They'll find the hardware stashed in the trunk, and if they trace the vehicle..." He left the rest unsaid.

Sugarman pursed his lips and blew. "It's still early morning. I could phone and report the car stolen. I've just got up and found it gone. After what happened around here last night—"

"And knowing your occupation, someone would put two and two together," Bolan finished. "No, we have to try to retrieve the vehicle. Make that me. I have no license, nothing to trace me to you. If I get away with it, then fine. If not, then I'm some idiot who took your car and it's up to me to get out of it."

"There'll be security footage of you and Justin," Stephanie pointed out.

Bolan allowed himself a smile. "Somehow or another, I figure that the Chinese and the Maltese are going to keep that to themselves. It's their war, and they don't want anyone else in on it. No, I'll try to retrieve your car. Meanwhile, Justin said something about knowing someone who can give us an address for that Internet travel company."

Sugarman nodded. "Yeah—Zak. I figure he'll like doing this." And when he noticed Bolan's inquiring expression, he elaborated, "Zak's always been one of the good guys. Straight as a die, as they say. But he had a brother who thought he was some sort of hotshot gangster and got killed by some rogue faction within the police. Only his gang thought it was the Mafia and the triads, and it all got a bit messy. Another Frank Gaunt story—he was in charge of the mopping-up operation. Zak's brother terrorized him, used his garage as a base. When things got really bad, Zak got visited by some overenthusiastic Chinese. They did nasty things to him, and he was so badly injured that he can't do anything as heavy as be a mechanic, which is a shame, because he was damn good. But he discovered computers, and he's got a knack for them. Did him a favor, in a way—he's got a really good Web-design and security business, now. Financially, he's never been better off. Inside, he's still bitter about what happened. Because it's Web security, he knows all the back doors, and he's never been averse to helping people like me and Justin. If the Chinese are involved, he'll only love it all the more."

Bolan grinned mirthlessly. "I like the sound of it the more that I hear about it. You track him down while I try and get the car back. And look after Stamp—he did good work last night," the soldier added.

Sugarman produced a street map of central London, and Bolan memorized the Soho streets, and how he would get there from the nearest subway station. Most of it he would know by sight...perversely, the hardest part to memorize was the winding route of suburban streets that would take him from the Sugarmans' house to the local subway station, which was on the right line to take him right in to where he wanted to go. While he pored over the maps, Stephanie reappeared with a jacket belonging to her husband.

"It's old, and should have been tossed out a long time ago," she commented, "but maybe it's just as well that I let him hang on to it."

Bolan could see what she meant as soon as he shrugged

into it. The jacket was in a mideighties style, and was extremely baggy. This meant that it avoided the tightness that would be a problem with other clothes belonging to Sugarman; more importantly, the bagginess would conceal the bulges of the Beretta and Desert Eagle that the soldier slipped into his waistband, under the untucked shirt and into the inner pocket of the jacket. As he took the hardware from the cabinet where Sugarman had hidden it when Tyler arrived, he could see the look of disapproval and fear cross Stephanie face.

"They may be necessary. Not for your police, because I'll go out of my way to avoid confrontation with them—at least, armed confrontation—but they're not the only problem. The gangs know what I look like, even if they have no idea who I am at the moment. I don't aim for them to get a chance to find out. Now, what the hell am I going to do about shoes?"

The Executioner discovered he was the same size as Sugarman, and slipped into a pair of running shoes. They felt comfortable, and were light enough to enable him to move with ease. If anything, it felt strange not to be wearing heavy combat boots. The only drawback, as far as he could see, was that they weren't exactly likely to pack a punch if he used them for kicking, and he might have to be mindful of that.

Leaving the subway train at Tottenham Court Road station, Bolan found that the daily routine of the West Enders was carrying on as usual. The crime scene where he and Stamp had hijacked the car had been thoroughly investigated and opened once more to allow the flow of traffic down the busy thoroughfare. He took a roundabout route through Soho Square and into the heart of the district, noting that some of the streets surrounding the club were still cordoned off for forensic examination, but for most of the district it was business as usual. The only thing betraying a major crime scene in the area was the increased amount of police, many of them discreetly armed. Bolan kept alert, ready to hurry out of there if recognized or stopped for any reason, but it seemed to be unnecessary. The major task for the police presence was to stop the rubberneckers who tried to stop to gawk at the scene of the carnage.

It wasn't a pleasant side to human nature, but it served the soldier well that morning. With the police thus occupied, it made it easier for him to locate Sugarman's car, and recon the area.

It was untouched in the side street. In normal circumstances, he would have expected it to have been towed for being in a no-parking zone, but the confusion of the morning had prevented the traffic cops from making their rounds.

So much the better. Bolan approached the car cautiously, checking for any hidden surveillance. Almost miraculously, it seemed as though the vehicle had been overlooked. Sitting on its own for so long, he would have expected it to have been targeted as a suspicious vehicle.

He unlocked the car with the remote locking trigger, and checked the vicinity before approaching the trunk. Lifting it carefully, just enough to view the interior, he was able to see that everything was as it had been left. He closed the trunk and got behind the wheel.

Switching on the engine, Bolan pulled away from the curb. He passed the end of the street where the firefight had taken place, being particularly careful with his driving as he passed the armed police standing guard. The last thing he wanted was to draw attention to himself. His fight wasn't with these people, and he intended to slip away unnoticed.

Out into Oxford Street, he turned right and headed for the

junction with Tottenham Court Road, then left and down toward Euston Road. His almost photographic recall of the route taken with Sugarman enabled him to get back to the house with only the one detour for an incomprehensible one-way system. The whole trip had taken just over two hours, and it was only just past midday when he pulled up in front of the Sugarmans' house.

But would they be any the wiser on where that job would take place?

The soldier entered the house and followed the sound of voices to the den. When he pushed open the door, he found Stamp sitting upright on the couch, with a large West Indian sitting awkwardly and uncomfortably beside him. The stranger had to be Zak. As the man looked up, Bolan could see that Zak's bloodshot and deep brown orbs reflected a lot of suffering, both in the past and right then. The depth of the pain became apparent when he levered himself off the couch to proffer his hand to the Executioner. Zak's movements were slow and awkward as he rose. And his knees were unsteady, suggesting that they, too, had been worked on in the past.

Zak inclined his head as Bolan took his hand, the clutch of long dreadlocks, shot through with white and gray, moving in time with his inclination. The man's grip, despite his old injuries, was firm—no-nonsense firm, suggesting that the older man was still shot through with a steel determination.

"Mr. Belasko," he said in a deep, resonating voice, "I've heard a lot about you. All of it good," he added.

"I've heard likewise," Bolan returned. "I hope you'll be able to help us."

"So do I," Zak murmured with an undertone that went beyond mere sincerity.

Sugarman was sitting in an armchair, leaning back. He gave every appearance of being relaxed, with his hands folded together. But the whiteness of his knuckles as he clenched his hands tightly was a giveaway as to how the tension was getting at him.

"You got the car all right, I assume," he said without preamble.

Bolan nodded. "It's outside. We were parked far enough away for it to escape any interest. The fact that we hijacked a vehicle to get away probably put them off the scent. All the hardware is intact, as well. But how are you doing?" he asked, turning to Stamp.

The big man grinned. His eyes were a little blurred, the pupils reduced to pinpoints. "The amount of junk Tyler's put me on for the pain, I feel like I could tackle the whole of the Mafia, the *mafiya,* the triads, the Maltese and the ghosts of Al Capone and the Kray twins with one hand tied behind my back." He chuckled. "I figure one arm's shot to shit—pardon the pun—for a while, but otherwise I'm feeling pretty good right now."

Bolan allowed himself a smile in return. "That's good, even if it is the painkillers talking."

He directed his attention back to Zak. "I take it that you've had the basic situation outlined to you?"

The West Indian assented. "The bastards need to be taken out. Sounds like you're the guy to do it. Whatever I can do will give me the greatest pleasure."

"Good. But is it possible?"

"Mr. Belasko, anything is possible if you just have the way in," Zak said with a humorless grin. "The trouble with these boys is they still have this insane notion of complete security. No such thing. People like me have to build the system for them, so we have to have a little back door in case it screws up. Whether it's the programming per se, or the security on that programming, it still amounts to one man having to have the access. Now, they think that everyone is so scared of them that they wouldn't dare try to break in after completing the work. But if you've done one, then you know how to look for the same result on others. You see?"

"Yeah, it seems a simple, basic principle. So can you do it right now?"

Zak allowed himself an indulgent smile. "Mr. Belasko, it's already done. While you were gone, I got the site address from these gentlemen, took a look at it and did some background. Didn't even have to crack security. I recognized the work—a guy called Devon, lives down in Tooting. Like any South Londoner, the boy's a fool. I phone him, and he thinks it's a straight business. No fear in his voice when I tell him what I want to know. He tells me like it's a normal business call, like I'm touting for work, looking to network. I know Devon, and he's chickenshit. If he didn't like me asking about them, the fear would have shown. I just had to wait for the good lady wife to leave, that was all," he added with a glance at Sugarman.

Bolan looked from Sugarman to Stamp. "Where is she?"

"Work," Sugarman said softly. "She's deputy headmistress at a primary school around here. I wanted her out of the way."

"I understand, believe me," Bolan replied. "She's safe. They haven't IDed you from yesterday—otherwise they would have been here. And if they know Justin from the security cameras, then we can safely assume it'll be him they chase first. She's a long way down the line, and we'll have things cleared up long before they can think of getting at her."

Of course, the soldier knew that this wasn't strictly true. There was always a chance that Stamp and Sugarman had been identified, and that Sugarman's wife would be chosen as a soft target to draw them out. But the gangs had been hit so hard and fast that, with the police presence in Soho also increased, it would slow the machinery of revenge enough for them to make their next strike.

Zak handed the soldier a piece of paper torn from a notepad.

"That's the address Devon gave me," Zak stated. "I know those buildings. High-tech security everywhere. Your image will be preserved in a whole lot of places. They have on-site security from hired firms. Mostly straight, and mostly slack, guys who want to have the easy life and wear a uniform, you know what I'm saying? But if these guys are in this building, the whole setup may be... Well, you don't need me to tell you, right?"

Bolan nodded. "I'll stay frosty."

"Whaddaya mean, you?" Stamp said indignantly. "Dude, I haven't come this far to be left behind."

"Justin, you've just had two pints of blood and half an illegal pharmacy pumped into you. You're junked to the eyeballs, reactions slowed if not erratic, and you won't be able to use one arm. I can't go in, face whatever's thrown at me, and watch your back," Bolan reasoned.

"You won't have to watch his back," Sugarman said quietly, "because I will."

The soldier turned to the detective. "I understand how you feel about this," he said, "believe me, I do. But you also know how I feel about your getting involved. It's not your strength, and you have—"

"It's Steph I'm thinking about," Sugarman interrupted. He

looked Bolan in the eye. "The way I see it, if you fail because you're outnumbered too heavily, then we go down anyway. So we go with you. And if we die? Well, I'm not kidding you here—I don't want to die. But if I get killed, then their problem is solved, and they won't come after Steph. She'll be a widow, sure, but at least she'll be able to find someone else, start over. If we don't back you up, and you fail because of that, she's as good as dead right now."

The soldier said nothing. There was a line of reasoning to Sugarman's argument from which the private detective wouldn't be shaken. And for their faults, he knew that he could rely totally on the integrity and courage of both men. If they hit hard, and with enough hardware, then maybe...

"Okay," he said. "You're giving me no choice here, but we may just be able to carry it off. We'll need to take time out briefly to plan, though. And I want your full attention—or as much as you can muster," he added as he looked at Stamp.

"This is my cue to leave, gentlemen," Zak said quietly. "May Jah speed you on the path of righteousness. I would offer to come with you, but I am a man of peace. At least, I was until my fool brother showed me the other path. And now, even though I would wish to leave that way and join you, I fear that I cannot."

The big West Indian struggled to his feet, and gathered his papers and attaché case from the couch beside him. Even his baggy tracksuit could do little to disguise the awkwardness of his movements, and the way that one of his feet remained at an unnatural angle as he stood. He grasped Stamp's hand, muttering "Strength, brother," then turned to Danny, who had risen from his own seat.

"Look, man," he said in a whisper, "you know that if anything happens, then Steph..."

Sugarman hugged the West Indian. "I know," he said simply.

Finally, Zak turned to Bolan. "Well, Mr. Belasko, you may be some man of mystery, but you make things happen. If anyone can see these guys through, you can. Take care, man, and keep the faith," he said, grasping Bolan's hand. Looking into his eyes, the soldier could see that Zak was almost envious of their ability to fight the evil head-on.

"I'll let myself out. You boys have a lot to discuss," he said, breaking away. His agonizing limp and shuffle—the first Bolan had seen of it—betrayed what he had been through in the past...and why he was driven to help them now.

They waited in silence until Zak had left, the click of the front door announcing his leaving. Then Bolan turned to Stamp—still wild-eyed on the couch, his upper arm and shoulder tightly dressed and bandaged—and Sugarman, who was almost drained of color beneath his thick mop of curls.

"Gentlemen, this may be a simple matter, or it may be difficult and violent. We can hope for the former, but we have to plan for reality. If we assume a worst case scenario, then we have as many eventualities as possible covered. I want us to hit the offices knowing exactly what we're doing. And the first thing is to make sure that we're prepared. Danny, I want you and Justin to find jackets as loose as this. We'll need cover for the hardware we're going to carry. And I also want blankets."

"Blankets?" Sugarman asked blankly.

Bolan grinned. "Yeah. Before we start planning, we need to empty the trunk of the car. We need to get 'tooled up' as Justin puts it, and you need to know how to use the weaponry. And I think it may look a little suspicious if we're seen in daylight carrying heavy-duty firearms into a terraced house."

8

Danny Sugarman was a quick study, and within half an hour Bolan had taught him how to use all the weapons that he had assembled in the trunk of the car. They had also been over tactics for best- and worst-case scenarios, and the soldier was certain that both men would know how to react and cover each other. They were his support team, and he trusted them to put themselves first in a moment of crisis. He was far better equipped to look after himself, and he would forge ahead while they retreated or held ground strategically.

Bolan and Sugarman returned some of the armament to the trunk, while their personal weapons remained in the house. During the relays to carry the inventory to its hiding place, Stamp began to loosen up. The pain deadened by the vast amount of painkiller coursing through his system, he flexed his aching limbs, finding that the only stiffness he suf-

fered was in the damaged arm and shoulder. He was a little
unsteady on his feet, but as he moved about the house he
began to feel stronger. He took the stairs two at a time, working his muscles back into life.

When Bolan and Sugarman had finished loading the
trunk, and had returned to the den, Stamp was standing in
the middle of the room, maneuvering his damaged arm into
the loosest jacket he'd been able to find in his less heavily
built partner's wardrobe. It was still tight on him, but would
enable him to hide some weaponry. There was another old
jacket waiting on the couch for Sugarman. As the detective
picked it up, Bolan could see the bloodstains left by Stamp
where he had lain earlier.

They checked their weapons. Bolan had the Desert Eagle
and Beretta, which were his weapons of choice. He'd also
hid away spare ammo clips, and some RGD-5 antipersonnel
grenades. A sheathed Tekna knife slid into the waistband at
the small of his back. A deep pocket in the right-hand side
of the jacket enabled him to secrete an SWA-12 assault shotgun. It made the jacket hang a little strangely, but he didn't
intend to be on view long enough for anyone to really notice.

Stamp took a Walther P-38, a Smith & Wesson M-4000
and a Wilkinson Sword hunting knife. He also managed to
pocket an MP-5, having developed a liking for the reliable
Heckler & Koch SMG during the previous night's engage-
ment.

Sugarman wasn't sure what to take, but on the recommen-
dation of both Stamp and Bolan for its relative ease of use, he
selected an Uzi and a Walther P-38. He also pocketed some of
Benny's stock of RGD-5s. Stamp had decided against grenades,
as they wouldn't be much use to him with only one good arm.

Following the Executioner's lead, both Stamp and Sugarman made sure they had plenty of spare ammo clips for their weapons.

"Ready?" Bolan asked when they were fully equipped.

"One last thing," Sugarman said. He left the room and returned with two tumblers of water. He said nothing in answer to Bolan's questioning glance, merely handing one to Stamp, who looked at him wonderingly. "Little something I got from Tyler before he left," Sugarman continued, going across to the medicines left heaped on the table. He sifted through, then produced a small brown bottle, from which he extracted four pills before handing two to Stamp.

"What's that?" Bolan asked.

"Benzedrine," Sugarman replied. "Look, Belasko, I can tell you don't like the idea of this, and to be honest with you, I'm not sure if it's the right thing myself. But I can tell you this—I knew I'd have to get involved, and I know enough about myself to realize that I may need a little help. And Justin needs it to counter the dope he's on for the pain. When I was a kid they called these bombers. You know why? I'll tell you. I had an uncle who was in the Polish free air force, flying with the British during World War II. That's how come I got born here and not Poland or Czechoslovakia. Anyway, he told me that everyone flying missions was on these, because they countered the fear, gave you the buzz and kept you awake. Not good to get hooked on, but they serve their purpose. And do I need that purpose now."

Bolan listened, then shrugged. "If you're sure, then I can't stop you," he said, knowing that prescription drugs used for such measures were still a part of combat, like it or not.

Sugarman popped the pills and washed them down with most of the contents of the tumbler. He screwed his face into a moue of distaste. "I hate taking pills of any kind, but I won't do it without them."

Stamp looked at Bolan and shrugged. "If it sharpens me up and makes me less of a liability, then I guess I'm the last one to complain, Mike," he said before popping the pills.

Both men placed their empty tumblers on the table and faced the Executioner.

"I figure that they should have kicked in by the time we get there," Sugarman said, "so I guess we should get going."

They left the room, Bolan in the lead. Sugarman stopped for one last, lingering look around the den, wondering if he'd ever see his home—or his wife—again.

THEY MADE the journey in silence, Sugarman driving. Bolan rode shotgun, and Stamp sat in the back seat, where he sprawled to make himself comfortable and save as much stress on his wounded arm as possible. Each man was wrapped up in his own thoughts, knowing that his death could be waiting at the end of the journey. For Bolan, this was an everyday occurrence. But for the two Britons, it was something that was frighteningly new.

It was just 3:30 p.m.—midafternoon in business terms— when they arrived in Docklands. The address Zak had given them was Terminal Tower at St Peter's Wharf. Named after the Docklands Light Railway Station that the new building overlooked, it had an aptly resonant name in the circumstances. The streets around the building were far from busy, but there were enough people passing by to take note of the car and its occupants.

"Where can we park out of the way?" Bolan asked.

Sugarman grimaced. "Probably nowhere around here. It's all controlled parking zones."

"So what do you suggest?" Bolan asked dryly.

"You're not going to like this, but I think we need to use the building's parking lot."

"You're right, I don't like it," Bolan agreed. "It could be dangerous getting stuck underground if the building is gang run, but I don't see that we have a better option."

"And they'll know we're coming," Stamp muttered from the back seat.

"Yeah, well, they'll have to live with that," Bolan growled as Sugarman negotiated a turn and drove down the slope leading to Terminal Tower's staff and visitors' parking lot. An overweight parking attendant in an ill-fitting blue uniform leaned out of a booth, not even bothering to put down his newspaper.

"Who are you here to see?" he asked in a disinterested voice.

"We're just here to see a few people about a trip to Indonesia, and we'd appreciate you keeping quiet about it." Bolan smiled, lifting the Desert Eagle out of its holster and directing it into the face of the startled guard. It was a snap decision. The man was slack, and no mob enforcer. It would be simple to intimidate him. Bolan's keen eyes noticed the guard's hand reaching for a button. "Not so fast," he snapped. "Try to raise an alarm, and you won't be alive when it goes off."

"I—I wasn't," the guard stuttered, his voice trembling in fear. His already pallid face was now chalk-white. "I was gonna raise the barrier, honest."

Bolan nodded. "That's good. Now just get out of that booth and wait calmly for me to get out and join you."

"Whatever you say, pal," the guard whispered hoarsely, scrambling out of the booth until he was standing in front of the car, arms half-raised, not knowing what to do.

Bolan slid out of the passenger seat and walked over to the guard. He kept the Desert Eagle as concealed as possible, but knew that anyone monitoring security cameras would already have seen red. Never mind. He could try to keep the exit cleared for later.

"Now, we're going into the booth, and you're going to raise the barrier and leave it raised. Then you follow me. Okay?"

Without reply, the guard moved slowly and nervously back to the booth, and pressed the button that raised the parking barrier. Sugarman drove through, and Bolan indicated for him to park near the exit. The detective complied, reversing so that the car would be able to drive straight out if they needed a swift exit. Meanwhile, Bolan ushered the guard out of the booth and across to the vehicle. He gestured for the trunk to be opened, and asked Sugarman if there was any rope or rags inside. The detective sifted under the hardware and came up with a blue nylon towrope, frayed but still heavy and strong.

"We're going to tie you up and put you in there," Bolan explained, indicating the trunk. "If all goes well, then you'll be let out safely when we've finished. You have nothing to fear if you play it down the line. Now, are there any cameras in the garage?"

The guard nodded, dry-mouthed and unable to answer.

"Where?" Bolan continued patiently as Sugarman bound the guard.

"One by the entrance, just past the booth...faces out to the street," the guard answered, indicating with his head. "And there's one on each level—three in this garage—at the bends on the roadway."

"Have we been spotted by now?"

The guard shrugged, shook his head wildly. "I don't know, honest I don't. I've never seen what they show. I don't think so, not unless they've got them fish-eye lenses on them. But I just don't know." There was a pleading edge to his voice. Bolan knew that he was telling the truth.

The soldier nodded. "Okay. Just keep quiet, and you'll be all right." He indicated for the guard to get into the trunk, and the man did this awkwardly, his weight and lack of fitness making it hard for him to balance with his hands tied, finding it hard to find any comfortable position on top of the hardware inside. Finally he was in, and he looked up at Bolan with wide, fearful eyes as the Executioner closed the trunk.

The three men walked across the almost deserted concrete surface of the underground parking area, dimly lit by inset lighting. Their footsteps echoed. Most of the offices in the building were empty or most of the employees came by public transport. Bolan hoped it was the former—that meant there was less chance of anyone getting caught in any crossfire.

The elevator and the emergency staircase were only a few yards apart.

"We taking the short way or the safe?" Stamp asked.

"Maybe both," Bolan replied. "We need to find out what floor they're on and if we've been seen. You guys go ahead," he said, gesturing to the stairs. "I'll catch up with you. Don't go out into the lobby until I join you," he added.

While Stamp and Sugarman entered the stairwell, both opting for their P-38s to draw as security, Bolan stood in front of the elevator, pressing the call button. He heard the mechanism whirr into action and the elevator descend. Keeping the Desert Eagle close to his thigh, he flattened himself to one side of the elevator doors, poised for when the car settled and the doors opened. He heard the car descend and then the squeal of the doors. He tensed; there was nothing. Pivoting in front, the soldier leveled the pistol at the opened doors, eliciting no response. He eased the pressure off the trigger and he stepped back.

Bolan reached in and pressed the button for the ground floor, ducking out before the doors closed and heading for the stairwell.

As he took the stairs three at a time, Stamp and Sugarman were waiting on the landing before the door to the ground-floor level. Bolan nodded.

"Okay, let's hit them when the elevator reaches—we should hear it," he added, mounting the last few stairs. The fire door before him was thick, but the walls weren't sturdy. He could hear the faint clanking of the elevator's machinery as it ascended and came to a halt, the doors beginning to open.

With the Desert Eagle up and ready, the soldier pulled open the fire door, taking in the lobby of the building with a raking glance. The elevator doors had opened onto an almost empty space, the only occupants of the lobby being a security guard in the same kind of rumpled blue uniform as the parking attendant, and a blonde with a fake tan and a tight blouse, her hair pulled back into a pert ponytail. The guard was paying no attention to the stairwell or the elevator, preferring to try to get better acquainted with the receptionist. She stood on the other side of a waist level counter from the guard.

They seemed innocent and harmless, but he couldn't take any chances. Moving out into the lobby, he leveled the Desert Eagle in their direction, Stamp and Sugarman fanning out behind him, providing cover and widening any possible angle of fire. The blonde caught the activity before the security guard, her eyes widening at the sight of the guns. She gave a little high-pitched scream of terror, making the guard turn suddenly.

"Oh, fuck," he said softly, color draining from his face.

"Do what I tell you and you won't get hurt," Bolan said calmly and with authority. "Miss, move out from behind the counter very slowly, keeping your hands where I can see them."

The blonde's bracelets jangled on her wrists as she kept her hands, shaking with fear, raised. As she came around the counter, Bolan could see that she was wearing a black microskirt, and she was teetering on four-inch stiletto heels. The blouse and skirt were tight enough—the blouse pulled agreeably tight by her raised hands—to show that she had no weapons on her.

"Now both of you come and stand in the middle here," Bolan ordered. As they hurried to do as he ordered, Bolan said over his shoulder, "One of you, check behind the desk for weapons, and look over the office in back."

Realizing that the soldier didn't want to mention names, Sugarman and Stamp exchanged glances before the big man walked across to check things out. While he did that, Bolan looked at the glass entrance to the lobby. Double doors made of smoked glass were set in a wall of the same. "You, go and lock those doors," he snapped to the guard, adding "Move it!" when the man failed to respond immediately.

The guard almost ran to the doors, fumbling with the electronic locks that secured the doors. Sugarman kept tabs on him, while Bolan questioned the woman.

"How busy is this building? Are most of the offices occupied?"

She shook her head, finding it hard to speak. When words did spill out, they were stuttering and hesitant.

"About ha-half the place is taken, but...mostly just as ac-accommodation. No-no one seems to come here much, just a few people. We've not been open long. Me and Tony—that's him," she added unnecessarily, indicating the guard, "we don't get much to do except stand around and chat and drink coffee. Where's Ralph?" she asked suddenly, looking around. "You haven't hurt him, have you?"

"If you mean the parking attendant, he's fine," Bolan told her.

The receptionist was about to speak, but the reappearance of Stamp, carrying two videocassettes, stopped her.

"Nothing much back there," the big man said perfunctorily. "They're not armed, and they don't seem that busy. There's video cameras for all floors, so I've pulled the plugs and taken the tapes for the garage and reception that could ID us," he stated.

"Okay, this looks like people live here, not mob-run business. But we'll make sure. Is there anything in that office?"

Stamp shrugged. "Phone, the video equipment, a few personal items."

"Okay, if you have cell phones, take them out now," he said, although it was directed at the security guard, as the tightness of the receptionist's clothing left no room for a cell phone to be concealed.

The security guard carefully reached into an inside pocket, as though scared that someone would think he was reaching for a gun, and extracted his cell phone. Following the soldier's gesture, he went over and put it on the reception desk.

"Now keys and your swipe cards—both of you," Bolan stated. Those, too, were placed on the desk. Bolan gestured, and the two hostages went into the small room at the rear of the reception desk. The soldier followed, keeping the Desert Eagle on them. It was purely for effect, as he had no intention of harming them.

He picked up a swipe card on the way and followed them into the room. He unplugged the phone and carried it out to the reception area, closing the door behind them and using the swipe to lock it.

From the sparsely lettered board by the double doors, the soldier could see that A-rave-daze—one of only seven companies listed in the multistory building—was on the sixth floor.

"Are we going to take the elevator or use the stairs?" Stamp asked.

"We should go on foot. It'd be safer," Bolan mused. "But are you going to be all right with that?"

The big man shrugged. "Dude, the amount of drugs I must have going around my system right now, I could probably float up there."

"Okay. We'll go on foot, but take it easy, okay?"

The emergency stairwell wound itself around the elevator, and they took the six floors in quick time, Stamp well able to keep pace. They passed no one on the way, although there were some sounds of activity as they passed the second and third floors. According to the board, there were no other companies on the sixth, so anyone they had to deal with directly was likely to be involved with the company they wanted.

Bolan took point when they reached the sixth, cautiously moving out into the corridor. It was empty, and he beckoned the others to follow him. Empty offices lined the semicircular corridor that wound around the building, with each office having glass-walled views of the Docklands area. Most office doors were closed and swiped shut, but those that were open showed empty floors and uncovered glass with the same opaque smokiness as the lobby.

When they reached the door marked A-rave-daze by a sedate and small silver plaque with black lettering, it was closed. Bolan listened at the door, but could hear nothing from inside—not even the sounds people made while trying to remain quiet. There was a stillness that suggested the office was empty.

"Let's hope this works. I don't want to make too much noise breaking in," the soldier said, almost to himself, as he tried the swipe card on the door's lock. "Well, what do you know?" he asked as the lock clicked open. "If I was renting this, I'd demand my money back."

He opened the door slowly, standing to one side of the jamb while Sugarman and Stamp stood to the other. There was a complete silence from within, and when he looked into the office, he could see it was unoccupied.

"Considering this is supposed to be where the business is based, they don't seem to be keeping too much of an eye on things, do they?" Sugarman said as he and Stamp followed Bolan into the office.

The carpet was the same as that in all of the empty offices. There were two desks. One housed a computer terminal; the other had two telephones and an ashtray. There were two cigar stubs in the ashtray, both long since extinguished. Each desk had one lavishly upholstered leather chair behind it. Whoever came here occasionally liked to repose in luxury. The only other piece of furnishing in the room was a gray metal filing cabinet.

"They can probably access most of the dealings on-line

from any terminal, and this is mostly for show. But just maybe they keep all the paperwork here. If we're lucky, and whoever heads this has a logical mind, it would keep all the paperwork away from the main body of the organization, and lessen the chance of incriminating evidence being pieced together." The Executioner moved toward the filing cabinet. "Justin, you and Danny see what you get on that terminal. I'm just going to have a little look in here."

He holstered the Desert Eagle and took the Tekna from its sheath in the small of his back. The finely tempered blade made short work of the locks on each of the drawers, and they were soon opened. Each of the four drawers contained a series of files, arranged in date, destination and alphabetical order for customer names. As he started to flick through the files, he noted that the company ran as a legitimate business alongside its less legal dealings, providing an effective smoke screen. In rave culture, it had found the right age and interest range of clientele to provide a strong cover.

As he read on, he heard the characteristic "Windows" musical motif as the computer booted up...and he heard something else. He turned rapidly to Stamp and Sugarman.

"We're not alone," he whispered. "I can hear someone on this floor."

Bolan gestured to Stamp and Sugarman to fan out on either side of the door, hugging the dividing wall between office and corridor. Luckily, there were no glass panels in the walls: at least the newcomer wouldn't be able to tell if anyone was waiting. The soldier opted to offer himself as a target, cutting down the chance of the two detectives' presence being guessed. He seated himself in the leather chair behind the terminal, hunkering low so that his presence could be seen, but the target offered was as small as possible. He had drawn the Beretta, which rested in his lap, out of view. It would be easy to bring to hand when required.

Nonetheless, it was a dangerous risk—not the type he usually indulged in, but necessary to give Stamp and Sugarman any time they may need to gain control of the situation.

They had moved swiftly and as near to silence as was possible. By the time the footsteps of the newcomer were clearly audible, they were in position. Whoever was coming toward the office made no secret of his or her approach. From the sound of the footsteps, it was a woman moving lightly and swiftly on heels that weren't necessarily that high, but were of enough substance to sound on the carpet.

She was unlikely to be a great danger against three, but Bolan was about to ease up. He gave an almost imperceptible shake of the head when Stamp shot him a questioning glance.

The woman appeared in the doorway, not seemingly surprised at finding the office open. She stood in the corridor, facing into the doorway. Bolan appraised her. The woman was about five-seven, a couple of inches taller in her heels. Muscular and shapely calves gave way to a knee-length black skirt, slit up the left thigh and tapering to a slim waist. She was well-defined and shapely, with long, raven-black hair flowing over her shoulders. She wore a tailored jacket that matched the skirt, with a blue T-shirt underneath. But it was her face that caught the Executioner's attention. She had olive skin and rich, dark brown eyes with an aquiline nose and full lips. The set of this normally stunning face showed a determination and barely concealed rage.

"This is A-rave-daze, right?" she began, the lightness of her tone belying the set of her features. "Holidays in the sun for those who just want to rave all night?"

Bolan nodded, waiting to see what her next move would be. She had a Gucci leather shoulder bag, and her left hand was clutching the strap tightly. She began to move her right hand toward the bag in a manner that struck Bolan's trained eye as exaggeratedly casual. The soldier tensed himself expectantly.

"I was wondering if you did bookings in the office, like, and not just over the Net, because if you do, I might be interested. Do you?" she asked, her voice hardening considerably on the last two words.

Stamp and Sugarman were poised with their P-38s up and ready, unable to act as she was still on the far side of the threshold. The big man shot another questioning glance at Bolan, who kept his eyes firmly on the woman. The Beretta nestled in his lap, and his fingers spread across the butt, instinct warning him to be ready to move.

"Maybe. Who wants to know?" he said, keeping his voice calm and low.

"I do, you bastard," she said in a chillingly low voice, almost growling as she pulled a Luger from the bag. She clicked off the safety and brought her left hand around to offer a supporting grip. She wasn't a professional, but she had made sure she learned something about handling guns.

The Luger was pointed at Bolan's head, the only part of him that presented a clear target. She would be unlikely to score a hit, even at such close range, if she was as unskilled as her movements suggested. But the soldier wasn't one to take chances.

He held up both hands—to show they were free, and also as a gesture of appeasement.

"Hey, you've got the jump on me," he said plaintively. "Just ask what you want."

"I will, you bastard, and you're going to tell me where my sister is...."

And then she committed the error for which he had been hoping. Believing him the only occupant of the room, she stepped over the threshold in order to close the door on the corridor.

As she did, both Sugarman and Stamp leveled their P-38s, the sound of the dual safety catches clicking off stopping her midstride. Her eyes flicked from side to side, taking in what had happened.

"Shit," she whispered.

"Now lower the gun," Bolan demanded. "Safety on. Then bend down very slowly and put it on the floor. And your bag." When she had complied, he continued, "Now come and sit down over here." He gestured to the other chair.

To Stamp, he said, "Better get that door closed before we have any other unwelcome guests."

While Stamp closed and locked the door, and Sugarman collected the Luger and the Gucci bag, the woman nervously perched herself on the edge of the chair, catching sight of the Beretta in the soldier's lap, and cautiously eyeing the other two men as they went about their business.

"It's okay—we don't run this little operation," Bolan explained. "In fact, we may have quite a lot in common. But you can't blame us for being a little suspicious of people who just pull guns without checking who we are first."

"I could say the same thing," the woman muttered.

Looking at her as she sat in front of him, Bolan could see that she was beautiful, but her face was lined with worry. Something seemed to have been bothering her for a while, and it seemed to center around this business scam.

"Here we go—have a look at this, Mike," Sugarman said, handing Bolan a driver's license that he had taken from the bag. "Otherwise she's clean."

The license told Bolan that she was one Traci King, aged thirty-six, and was resident in Peckham, South London. She had also been less aged by worry when the photograph on the license had been taken, less than two years before.

"So, Miss King—Traci—why don't you tell us why you're here?"

She looked at each of the three in turn, as though trying to figure out if they were trustworthy. Bolan doubted that he would find anyone with a gun trustworthy, but she didn't really have a lot of choice. She was alive, and she hadn't even been touched. That had to tell her something.

It seemed that it did, for she began to speak, hesitantly at first, directing her attention to Bolan.

"I've got a sister—well, I had a sister. I suppose I still have, but it's the not knowing that's the worst part. I guess that isn't making much sense, but... Okay, it started with Elena—that's my sister—wanting to go on a holiday with her friends. She's over ten years younger than me, and Mom and Dad always doted on her a bit much, you know? That's my fault, because I fell in with some people who thought they were a bit...unsavory. Lived with this guy who's in Wormwood Scrubs now, doing ten for robbery with assault.

"Anyway, that doesn't matter except that they kept Elena a bit sheltered. So when she finally got out from under their thumb, she really did. Raving and that, doing E and staying away for days at a time. She's done Ibiza and the Balearics, and she was looking to hit the hippy trail. She used to go to that club where they had the shootings last night, and she told me about this holiday she'd booked over the Net. It was this company, and when she booked on her own, she got some e-mails from someone—all that 'friend of a friend' crap, asking if she wanted to earn a bit more cash for her holiday. Turns out this bloke she was seeing put her onto the company, and maybe put them on to her, you know?

"So anyway, she went a couple of months back. No postcards—no surprise. But she didn't come back. And when I asked some of her friends, after Mom and Dad got worried, they hadn't seen her over there. Well, the police were useless, and my parents didn't know what to do, so I decided I'd do a bit of looking for myself. Elena's a good kid, but really stupid when it comes to things like. Well, she hasn't been around enough."

"And you have, by the sound of it," Stamp interjected. "To cut a long story short, you asked a few old friends of your own, and that's how you got the gun...and learned how to handle it, right?"

King nodded. "Yeah. I just want to know what you've done with her...before you get rid of me, as well."

"I told you, we're not with the people behind this, although we know who they are—"

"That slimy Maltese pimp and his Chinese friends," she interrupted emphatically. "I know him, all right. When I kept turning up at the club, and then the lap-dancing club, he got suspicious of me—"

"Well, I can't imagine you were too subtle about it," Sugarman said wryly. "You don't exactly make much of a pretense at stealth."

The woman flashed him an angry glare. "Look, I don't know anything about how you're supposed to do this, but if my sister's dead, the bastard who did it is going to pay."

There was a fire and venom in her voice, a determination that struck a chord in the soldier.

"We're not here to judge you or your methods," he said carefully. "But you've uncovered a lot for someone who's been tagged by the bad guys."

King gave Bolan a wry grin of her own. "Yeah, well, being a woman sometimes has its advantages. I reckon I would have been dead by now if I'd been a guy, but the Maltese are still so old-fashioned that they only see women as whores or moneymakers of some kind. The Chinese are different. They would have killed me, but I had something over Artruro that they couldn't better."

"Which is?" Bolan asked, interested.

She gave a small triumphant laugh. "The stupid, evil old bastard wants me for himself. I'm not getting any younger, but I'm not bad for my age. When I worked out that a lot of the guys working at the dance club use to be in and out of the lap dancer all day, I knew that there had to be a link. So I turned up there, and of course they got suspicious—some woman on her own in a place like that? I was either a whore trying to work on their territory, or I was after something. They knew I wasn't police because they've got them sewn tight. So I made out like I was trying to get back into dancing after being out a while—spun them some story about a guy I was with who didn't like me doing it, but now he was off the scene, all that—and I'd heard that this was the club to come to work.

"Guys are such suckers. I asked Artruro for a private audition. It's amazing how you can sweep away a man's suspicions just by letting him see a little skin."

"Is that how you found out that the office for the Net company was here?" Bolan asked.

"Indirectly, yeah. When I said I was thinking about going on one of those holidays, Artruro laughed and told me that it wasn't for the likes of me, and that I might not like what happens. But the thing is, he kept referring to it as something else—as Marduke, not A-rave-daze. So it didn't take much brain for me to look up Marduke Limited at Companies House and find this address. I came here a few days ago, and it was empty. I tried to get in, but that security guard had followed me. So I thought I was in luck when I got here and there was no one around in the lobby. And then when the door was open and you were sitting there..."

Bolan nodded. "So how did you get into the building?"

"Through the garage, of course. That's where I parked." Suddenly it dawned on her. She said slowly, "What have you done with the fat bloke who works down there?"

"He'll be fine," Bolan said shortly.

Then he turned to Stamp and Sugarman. "But that does bring home the point that we should tidy up here and get the hell out. Right, gentlemen?"

"I'll agree with that," Stamp said, moving to the computer. "Give me a couple of minutes, and I'll sort this so we can look at their files in peace."

Bolan made way toward the big man and directed Sugarman to gather together as many of the files from the filing cabinet as he could carry. Some of these he handed to King.

"Look, if you're not with the Maltese or the Chinese, who the hell are you?" she asked as she was loaded up.

"Interested parties, no more, no less. Let's just say that incident at the dance club was only the beginning."

King bit her lip and looked at Stamp's dressed wound as he sat transferring files to diskettes. "Look, I just want to find my sister, not get caught up in some sort of war."

Bolan stopped and looked into her eyes. "Lady, as soon as you decided to start looking, you signed up for the war, whether you like it or not."

"Done," Stamp said, cutting across the exchange. He brandished a pile of diskettes.

"Okay. Let's get going," Bolan told them.

He opened the office door and scanned the corridor. It was empty. He swiftly moved to the stairwell, and checked the landing before beckoning the others to follow. The soldier led them to the ground floor, opting to leave the security guard and the receptionist secured in the small back room. Those seeking to leave the locked building at the end of the working day would discover them soon enough.

They reached the basement parking level, and the soldier opened the fire door carefully. There was little chance of anyone being around, but even the smallest chance demanded caution. There was no truly safe way of scouting around the heavy door, so he had to take a chance. The underground parking area was empty, the only other car having arrived since their entrance being a battered Ford Capri painted bright yellow.

"Yours?" Bolan asked as they made their way across the concrete.

King nodded.

Bolan took the files from the woman and put them on the back seat of Sugarman's car. "You drive outside and wait, then follow us," he told her. When she looked at him questioningly, he explained, "I'm going to free the attendant, and I don't want him to be able to identify you or your car."

She hurried to the Capri, looking back at them over her shoulder as though she still didn't quite trust them. She got into her car and drove out of the parking area. The men watched her go before turning to the trunk. Bolan opened it and hauled the attendant, blinking at the sudden light, to his feet. The man's legs had cramped from restricted circulation, and he sank to his knees. Bolan lifted him, and held him until he felt as though he was stronger on his feet.

"Okay, now listen carefully," Bolan said. "We overpowered you, and you didn't get a good look at us. You could be dead now, but you're not. Remember that, as you may not get lucky a second time."

The attendant nodded. "What about this?" he asked, feebly gesturing with his bound arms.

"Call it an ingenuity test. See if you can get up to the ground floor, free the guard and the receptionist and get them to untie you."

With which, he got into the passenger seat of the car. Sugarman had already gunned the engine, and Stamp was in the back seat. The car pulled away with a squeal of tires, making the attendant jump back, stumble and nearly lose his balance.

As they left the garage, he was turning and making his way to the elevator.

"That should keep him occupied for a while," Stamp mused. "But what about this woman? Should we trust her?"

"I figure we should keep her on side. She may not be of much practical use, but the last thing we want is a loose cannon while we're trying to cut through the crap. I want to close these guys down, and I want those Serbs. Anything that gets in the way needs stopping. And if she's got this far, then she's not easy to stop."

"Yeah, I reckon you're right there," Stamp muttered, watching the yellow Capri, through the rear window, as it followed them out of Docklands.

10

Detailed examination of the paper files and those on disk revealed the full extent of the operation within a matter of an hour. The security shown by Artruro Sartini's operation was incredibly slack, and Bolan found it hard to believe that he had maintained a working relationship with the triads for even the short time that he had. From his own experience with them in the past, the soldier knew how intolerant they were of anyone whose actions would endanger the smooth running of the business.

They didn't take Traci King back to the house. Instead, they headed for the office on the main drag, parking on a nearby side road. King managed to find a space for her garishly colored car near to them. Sugarman had been careful to check that they weren't tailed from Docklands, but still felt uneasy about such a conspicuous vehicle being identified with them. As she joined them at their vehicle, Bolan loaded her up with the file folders, leaving his own hands free in case they were attacked. It was highly unlikely, but caution was always the watchword. Besides which, it was important that the least capable fighter be kept out of the fray.

The quartet made it to the office without drawing any attention to itself, and once inside the office they were able to relax a little.

"We need to get through this mass of paperwork quickly," Bolan stated. "We can't rely on the element of surprise any longer. They have video of us, and they'll know from descriptions that we were the ones at the office. It's only a matter of time before they track us. And even if we hit them now, they'll be waiting."

Sugarman made coffee while Stamp booted up the computer and attempted to access the disks. He had some knowledge of computers, and was quite prepared for a series of security codes that might need breaking before he was able to access the information.

However, he had reckoned without Traci King. The raven-haired beauty was looking over his shoulder as the screen flashed the need for a password.

"Try 'Marduke,'" she said softly.

Stamp frowned and keyed in the word. It worked.

"How did you know that?" he asked with a hint of suspicion.

She barked a laugh that was laced with disgust. "You don't know how close I've had to get to that filth Arturo. I know how his mind works. He uses the registered name of the company as a password because his memory's so bad he wouldn't remember anything else."

"Are you sure it doesn't have any other significance?" Bolan asked, looking up from the file folders.

The raven tresses shook. "No, I'm pretty sure of that. It has that name because it was bought off the shelf as a company, and it was probably just the day for anything beginning with *m*," she replied.

They returned to silence, distributing a selection of file folders between Bolan, King and Sugarman, while Stamp keyed his way through the files on disk. When they had finished and pooled their information, the whole picture began to emerge.

Sartini had been in financial trouble. The amount of money he'd been paying as bribes to both the police and to the local authorities to insure the lap-dancing club was converted and opened had been excessive, and had come at a time when his other illicit businesses had been the victim of both a legal clampdown by those sections of the police not in his pocket, and by the incursion of other gangs onto his territory. One of these had been a triad, led by a Lin Ho, whose name Bolan recognized.

"Lin Ho was an enforcer in the San Francisco area who rose through the ranks. His trademark is to be silent and seemingly inoffensive, yet he's a callous and bloodthirsty assassin. I've seen some of his work. When he has time, he'll make a contract last. The victim will probably be insane from the pain before he or she actually dies. If he was put in command of this projected takeover, then an initial alliance is very much his style. Let Sartini make mistakes, let him think he has the upper hand and that Lin is a fool. Then the eventual death of the Maltese is all the sweeter for Lin."

"Charming bloke," Stamp mused.

King shook her head. "Couldn't happen to a nicer geezer, believe me."

With Sartini in debt, and accepting the overtures of the

triad to join forces, it was imperative that he come up with an operation that would enable him to continue his own specialized business with that of his new business partners. As he had just acquired a controlling interest in several regular nightclubs in the area, including the one frequented by King's sister and the missing Samantha True, it seemed perfect to invent a travel agency that specialized in holidays to a clubber's favorite destinations. Especially as those locations dovetailed neatly with the eventual destinations of both the drugs and the women that were his cargo. Mules and possible female stock to run alongside that which he already had in his possession.

It was interesting that the view of both Stamp and Sugarman, from their own investigations, had been that it was Sartini who had made overtures for the merger between the Maltese and the triads. The paperwork and computer files made it obvious that he had been maneuvered into this action by the work of Lin Ho. It showed the subtlety the triad overlord could bring to his affairs, and was a warning to all of them that the fight ahead wouldn't be a straightforward experience.

The day-to-day running of the business was simple. Some flights and holidays were legitimate. In fact, they ran at a rate of three to one in favor of the strictly aboveboard. That provided a nice cover for the real business, and also paid the overheads of the company, enabling a set of legal books to be kept. The flights used for both illegal and legitimate passage were chartered, through a company in which Sartini and his brothers were major shareholders. At the end of the line, hotel accommodation was booked for all customers in hotels that were part or wholly owned by triad concerns. It was from here that some customers failed to return. In view of

the beach-bum culture of the region and of the rave genera-
tion that followed the trail, such things weren't unheard-of.
That was all the excuse the local police needed to leave the
matter alone. Of course, the drugs could easily be muled past
customs from a charter flight, as it was a simple matter of
arranging for the right person to be on customs duty. At the
English end, it was perhaps harder to achieve. However, a
file of payments to customs officials at Heathrow told its own
story.

Once past the basic overview of how the business ran, the
files made for grim reading, both on paper and on disk. Client
files named customers, destinations and who was legitimate
and who either a mule, or a shipment, or both. Amounts of
money on the head of each customer were carried in U.S. dollars, Hong Kong dollars and sterling, with a full inventory of
both drugs and girls shipped over the past eighteen months.

"Stop—stop right now!" King cried suddenly as another
passenger flight list scrolled off the screen. "Back a bit..."

Stamp cursored back until the full inventory for that flight
was centered on screen. There, three-quarters of the way
down the page, was the name Elena King, along with the
price she had paid and an additional figure that they knew
represented a street value for a drug consignment.

"She was a mule," Sugarman muttered. "I wonder if she
knew... Look, she's cross-referenced."

Stamp followed the cross-reference until he found her
name on a hotel registry booking list.

"Look at that," he whispered. "She was booked for two
weeks, but went after two days. That's a bit quick, even for
a runaway. And there's a note on there...'payment deferred.'"

"The bastard used her, then sold her," King said coldly.
"I'm going to kill him."

"Wait," Bolan told her. "Don't let your anger get the better of you. Save it and use it. There are other 'payment-deferred' tags in here. It's possible she may be in a holding pen of some kind, not yet passed on to her eventual destination."

"They do that?" Sugarman asked, amazed.

"It's not unknown. If a customer can't pay, or if they're expecting a glut of orders, then they need some 'stock' at hand. I've seen this before."

"Go on...quickly," King urged. "I need to see something else—anything."

Stamp continued to trawl through the computer records while the others took the file folders. After the outline of the business, and the detailed transaction records, came the biggest surprise: Arturo Sartini had used the computer in the A-rave-daze office to keep records of all his staff. Everyone on the payroll, from the lap dancers in the club, including King, through to the enforcers he had brought in as mercenaries, were detailed, their names and addresses next to their salaries.

"I'll give him ten out of ten for accounting efficiency, but zero out of ten for intelligence," Stamp said as he scrolled through the file. "They're all here—and there are some Serb names, Mike."

Bolan left his seat and read through the file over the big man's shoulder. There were seven Serb mercenaries working for the Maltese gang boss, and any two of them could be the killers Bolan sought. He smiled.

"Got them. We know where they work, and where they live. Justin, I want a backup on this. Is there someone you can trust on the local police?"

Stamp nodded. "Yeah, there are a couple of guys on the local team that we know are straight. They're far enough away from the vice and drugs teams at the Met not to be tainted in any way, or to have things disappear from their desks when they're not looking. Why?"

"Because we're going in, and we may not come out. If we don't, I wouldn't like to see all this go to waste. Someone should nail this scum, even if we don't."

"I'll agree with that," Sugarman said, coming over. "And I think I know exactly where we can get them." He held a file in his hand, which he waved excitedly. "It's in here—the complete business structure at the top of the organization. He's a compulsive for putting it all down on paper!"

"Probably thinking of writing his memoirs in exile on the Costa Del Sol," King said bitterly. "He's got an ego a mile wide."

"Most of them have," Bolan commented. "And that's what tends to be their downfall. Why don't you take us through it?"

Sugarman took a deep breath, framing his reply carefully. "It goes like this. Uncle Artie likes to keep his records separate from the business headquarters, which is why he found the office so convenient—and probably why it's rarely frequented. After all, he wouldn't want just anyone snooping around in there, would he? Anyway, all his business is dealt with from the lap-dancing club. That's part of the reason he paid out so much in bribes to get it up and running. At the rear of the club, he houses all his heavies who are on duty, and he's had a strongroom built into the premises for any cash, guns or drugs that he wants to hand for specific tasks. It's well hidden, according to the plans, but not when someone is actually kind enough to leave those plans out in the open for you. So there you are, his complete operation in one place. Take that out of the equation, and you've eliminated his threat."

Bolan considered that. "That's good, particularly with the plans to guide us. But the Maltese are only half of this problem."

A sly grin lit up Sugarman's face. "Yeah, I know. But that's where Uncle Artie being such a stickler for putting things down on paper comes in a bit useful."

Bolan began to see the light. "You mean to tell me he's actually put Lin Ho's center of operations down there?"

Sugarman nodded. "Not directly, but he's got a chain linking all his finances to Lin Ho's and the triad banks. I guess it's so that he's able to keep track of everything that comes and goes through his hands, in case they try to cheat him. But a byproduct of it is that he's given us their center of operations on a plate. And it's the most clichéd trick of them all."

Bolan laughed shortly. "A Chinese restaurant in Chinatown. The ultimate triad hide-in-plain-sight. I should have guessed as much from someone with Lin Ho's twisted sense of humor."

"Yeah, and it's not a bad restaurant, either. I've taken Steph there a few times," Sugarman said with some bemusement.

Stamp frowned and leaned over to check the name on the file. "Damn! I took my last date there," he muttered.

Bolan looked at the name on the file: Hoo Hing. He remembered passing it the previous afternoon, when he had been trailing the Serbs through Soho before losing them. That had been just before he'd caught sight of the triad gunmen he had seen back in San Francisco. Yeah, it made perfect sense.

"So the money laundering, the white slavery and the dope running all revolve around two particular centers," Bolan said decisively. "That shouldn't make things too difficult."

"Tell me why I don't feel that way?" Stamp said uneasily. "Mike, these are heavy-duty dudes, and we aren't. You are, but the rest of us?"

Bolan sat behind the detectives' desk, so that he faced Stamp, Sugarman and King.

"I'm not asking you to be part of this if you don't want to be," he said simply. "You don't have the training and experience, and it wouldn't be fair of me to expect you to follow. But you do all have raw courage, and if you follow my game plan, you won't be in the front line when it goes down. I can handle that. All I ask is some reconnaissance work and maybe some backup."

"You know we're behind you on that," Sugarman said.

"Good. The way I see it, the initial target is the Maltese base of operations. I have my own particular reason for wanting to take that out, as you know, but it will be the easier of the two targets. The Maltese and their mercenaries are sloppy. The triad isn't. Traci, I need something special from you."

She looked at Bolan with a mixture of trepidation and excitement. He guessed that she knew what he was about to ask.

"I stand a better chance of getting into the club and the heart of the operation without any trouble if I'm with you. They know you there, and know what Artruro thinks of you, right?"

"Yeah." She nodded firmly. "I doubt if they'd even look at you twice if we just breezed in there like I'd never been away. Yeah, I'll do it."

"Thanks. You're one brave lady, Traci. Don't think I don't appreciate what you're doing," Bolan said simply.

Then he turned to Stamp and Sugarman. "As for you guys, I want you to go to Hoo Hing and keep watch. Can I borrow a cell phone?"

"Yeah, mine's in the desk," Stamp told him. "I left it there a couple of days ago. It might need charging, but there might be enough in it."

Bolan reached into the drawer and examined the cell phone. The charge was low, but it should be enough for his needs.

"It'll do. I want you to monitor the restaurant so that you can tell me the situation when I leave the lap-dancing club. I'll call you for a report on my way over."

"Uh, what if you don't call?" Sugarman asked after an awkward exchange of glances between the two detectives.

"If I don't call, then I'm not coming, and there's no sense worrying about it," the soldier said matter-of-factly. "Don't even think about going in there on your own. I know Lin Ho, and I know how well he'll have his men trained. If I don't get out alive, then go to the police. I figure they'll already know about what's gone down at the club," he added.

Sugarman looked at his watch. "It's coming up to seven. Shit, it's only been twenty-four hours since—"

"Yeah, I know. Sometimes it can seem like a lifetime," Bolan interrupted. "But there's still work to be done. Gather up the files and get the disks. Before anything else, we need to get this material to your local contact. That way we have some kind of backup to nail these bastards if we don't make it."

"And then?" Stamp asked.

"Then we find somewhere remote where we can get a full inventory for the battle ahead. Traci, you may have to learn something about the hardware we'll be carrying."

"I'll do it, don't worry," she said in small voice, nervous but determined.

"I know you will," Bolan answered. "I hope you won't have to use any of it, but if you do, it might just save your life...maybe even mine.

"Okay, let's go."

11

Sugarman took the car on a main road out of Leytonstone, past one roundabout and down an arterial road to another. On the way, he stopped off outside a police station and disappeared inside with a sealed envelope on which was written a specific name and a brief note explaining that it wouldn't be necessary to open the envelope until the following day.

He left the station and got back into the car.

"Well?" Bolan asked.

"He's out on a job. It's on his desk—I know because I put it there myself after talking to his chief. He thinks I'm a waste of space, so he won't bother opening it. It'll be safe until morning."

Once back on the arterial road, he rattled over a cattle grid and took a side road that led into a piece of deserted woodland. They exited the car, and Bolan took a good look around. It was summer, warm and still light. Yet, despite the fact that he could hear the traffic buzzing distantly over the evening air, the piece of woodland seemed deserted and desolate.

"You sure we won't be disturbed?" he asked.

Sugarman shook his head. "No one ever comes here. It's not really pretty enough. Until a few years ago, there still used to be herds of cattle from local farms that roamed freely here—part of some old law allowing right of way. That's why they've still got the cattle grids in the road back there. But when they built the M11 Link Road, the cattle disappeared, and this area got free of cow shit. Still doesn't attract hikers and the nature crowd, though."

Bolan nodded. Sugarman had given the matter of a quiet area in which to load up, and teach Traci King the rudiments of the inventory, no little thought. They were still in the heart of suburban London, and yet he had found them an isolated spot in which to run through the weapons and the plan.

Stamp, under Bolan's orders, kept watch while the soldier opened the trunk of the car and started to run through the hardware contained within. King's eyes widened when she saw the range of weapons. She'd never seen so much destructive power in one place. But she overcame her shock, the thought of her missing sister spurring her on, and listened carefully to the Executioner's concise instructions. Within twenty minutes, she knew how to handle most of the weapons in the trunk, if not like an expert, at least well enough to use them in a combat situation.

Bolan gave her a 9 mm Czech-made CZ-75 semiautomatic pistol, a couple of RGD-5s and an AKSU assault rifle. It was a particularly good weapon for her, as the short barrel and folding stock made it a much more portable—and more easily concealed—version of the AK-74 while having much the same potential as an assault weapon.

And Bolan had every intention of taking the offensive.

Sugarman took over watch while Stamp replenished his ammo supplies and took up the weapons he had carried before. He returned to watch while his partner did likewise.

There were some guns left in the trunk that they wouldn't be using. They would have to be dumped, so that the car would be clean if it was found by the police and searched while they were absent. Bolan stripped the guns, leaving them devoid of firing pins and other relevant parts, rendering them nothing more than useless shells. He dug two shallow holes and buried the body of the weapons in one, and the stripped parts in another. Then he took the grenades and the explosives, and climbed a tree, placing them in a hollow that couldn't be seen from the ground.

"Remember where these are, all of you," he said as he climbed down. "If we get out, first chance we get, we come and get them. They should be safe enough for now, but I don't want them left too long where they could be found."

"What about if we don't get out?" Sugarman asked.

Bolan fixed him with a steely glare. "I don't consider that an option, and neither, in truth, should you," he replied.

Now they were ready.

"You know the basic plan," Bolan said briefly. "When we reach Soho, it's probable that it'll be crawling with police. After the events of last night, I'd be surprised if it wasn't. But if my recon earlier today is anything to go by, then they'll be trying to keep a low profile and let business proceed as usual. Make no mistake—they'll be armed, and they will be prepared to shoot. And from their point of view, we're just as much the bad guys as the Maltese or the Chinese. So we try to avoid them, and if we have to engage, we try to take evasive action, and avoid unnecessary death. They aren't our enemy, but the amount of hardware we're all carrying makes us theirs, unfortunately.

"So the rule of thumb is conceal it until the last possible moment. Danny, I want you to take the car into Soho as much as is possible, and park up somewhere equidistant to the restaurant and the lap-dancing club. We want somewhere relatively inconspicuous, but also easily accessible. With the number of alleyways and back streets in the area, it shouldn't be that difficult," he added.

"There, we separate. Traci and I will proceed to the club, and you guys go to recon the restaurant and wait to hear from us. The only thing left to say is good luck, and keep it frosty, people. The only chance we have is if we keep our heads and let them screw up. Let's go."

IT WAS JUST past eight when they entered Soho. In the balmy early evening, the streets were thronged with tourists and native Londoners set for a night on the town—perhaps even a night to remember. The ravages of the previous evening hadn't deterred them. Indeed, for some the notion of becoming involved in similar situations may even have been a spur. These were people for whom violence had little more than the aspect of a scene in a movie. It was an excitement in an otherwise dull life. The blood, and the stench of death, wasn't something that was real. Despite the presence of more police on the streets than usual, it was almost a carnival atmosphere.

But not in the car that Sugarman piloted through the traffic. The four occupants were somber, in contrast to the atmosphere around them. They had a job to do, and in their own ways they knew what violent death was about, knew the cost of blood and bullets. It wasn't a matter for lightness of heart. If they were to make it through this in one piece, let alone avoiding capture by the police in the aftermath, they would need their wits about them and absolute concentration.

The car passed the end of the road where the previous night's shootout had taken place. Despite the barriers and the police presence, there were still a few who paused on their way along the street to take a look at the site before being impatiently moved on by the law.

"This place is crawling with the police," Stamp murmured. "Not just uniforms—they've got a lot of plainclothes people wandering the streets."

"How do you know?" Bolan asked. He had arrived at a similar conclusion, but wanted to hear Stamp's reasoning.

The big man allowed a smile to crack his face for the first time that evening. "Come on, Mike. We've been around them long enough, in one way or another, to be able to tell. It's like an instinct, isn't it? I bet Traci can tell, as well."

He turned to the woman sitting next to him, who was nervously looking out the window.

"Yes, I reckon you're right about that," she almost whispered. "You can tell they're there, even when you can't see them."

"Good," Bolan said flatly. "Then we'll all know who not to kill when the time comes. Remember who the enemy really is."

Sugarman had stayed silent throughout this exchange, concentrating on negotiating through the traffic. The flow of vehicles through the tightly packed streets had reduced to a crawl as the crowds spilled onto the streets, and cars that took their chance coming out of side streets almost collided with impatient drivers who were trying to snatch precious feet and inches of road space. Finally, as he indicated and swung off the main road, narrowly avoiding a motorcyclist, Sugarman spoke. His voice was soft but strained, taut with tension.

"This is about right to keep us between the restaurant and the club. The only problem is if we'll find a parking space or not."

The narrow side street led onto a dead end alleyway, where the recessed doorways of advertising and video production companies were closed for business, leaving it a safe haven—in theory—until morning. Sugarman pulled up at the end of the alley, in front of a doorway for Beard Brothers Productions, with Adult Video Network written on a small card by a doorbell.

"Lovely place you've picked," King said coolly as she got out of the back, followed by Stamp.

"It serves a purpose." Sugarman shrugged. He locked the car after they all exited the vehicle.

"Okay, people, you know what to do," Bolan said quietly as they assembled at the head of the alleyway, facing the street. "Good luck," he added to Sugarman and Stamp.

"You, too," the big man acknowledged. "Remember the memory on the cell phone. Danny's number one on there. We'll be waiting for you," he added.

Bolan nodded briefly and, taking King by the arm as though they were a couple on a night out, he turned and walked away.

Toward the club, and a date with destiny.

"LOOKS SO BLOODY innocuous, doesn't it?" Sugarman said quietly to his partner as they stood across the street from the restaurant. A giant neon sign naming it Hoo Hing in both English and Cantonese ran between the second and third floors. It had five altogether, including the ground, and on each diners were packed in as fast as they could be emptied out. The staff had a reputation for brusqueness, but the food was good and it was cheap. As a Cantonese equivalent of a North American fast-food restaurant in terms of rapid service and consistency, it had proved to be a draw to both locals and tourists alike.

"Yeah, but what better front, if you think about it," Stamp replied, flexing his bandaged shoulder. The jacket hid the dressing, but he was aware that the painkillers were beginning to wear off.

"It giving you grief?" Sugarman asked, noticing the expression on his partner's face as he flexed.

Stamp grimaced. "Yes and no. I could've done with a couple more painkillers, but all it's doing is making me feel a little testy about the bastards who did it to me. I figure that maybe that'll come in handy a bit later."

Sugarman nodded briskly. "Yeah, I reckon that maybe we'll need all the adrenaline rush we can get."

The restaurant had a revolving door with swing doors to either side. A constant stream of people flowed in and out. Both men knew that the chances of gaining entrance without being spotted would be improved immeasurably by this, but also that the crush of people would make it hard to pick out enemies, or any who were watching. The floor-to-ceiling windows on each level showed how busy and packed the restaurant could be. Even without the illegal earnings that it fronted, the business had to be a legitimate goldmine in its own right.

"We need to get off the street, make sure we don't get noticed too easily," Stamp said, looking around. There was a bar almost directly opposite the front of Hoo Hing, with a vacant table at the window. The big man grinned at his partner. "What do you know, Dan—it's got our name on it. We can keep to ourselves until Belasko calls, keep an eye on the place and get a medicinal double down our necks."

"Shit, we don't want to get pissed," Sugarman cautioned.

Stamp shook his head. "I know, Dan, but I could kill a beer with a Jack Daniel's chaser. Down the JD in one, then make the beer last. Don't tell me that doesn't sound appealing."

Sugarman shrugged. "Yeah, I guess it does. You grab the table, I'll get the drinks."

As they entered the bar, he whispered under his breath, "The condemned man drank a hearty breakfast...."

"LISTEN, MATE, you don't have to overdo the act," King whispered at Bolan as they made their way down the crowded street. The soldier still had hold of her arm and was gripping it tightly. So tightly that it was beginning to hurt.

"Sorry," the Executioner said, relaxing his grip. "I just don't want us to get separated."

"You mean you don't want me to turn tail and run," she corrected.

Bolan spared her a wry grin. "Maybe..."

"Look, I would have done that a lot earlier today if I didn't want to do this," she told him in an undertone. "I don't like shooters, and I don't like playing with them. But I like those Maltese bastards a whole lot less. And they know who I am now. It wouldn't take them long to put two and two together, even if I did take off. So I might as well face up to it now. I'm in this for the long run, just like you."

"Good, because we're nearly there, and I need you to keep it together," Bolan explained. "There's not much chance of the same staff being on—especially as most of them are dead or wounded after our little skirmish yesterday evening. But they might recognize me from videotapes if I just walk in there with you. I need to keep myself hidden as much as possible."

"Yeah, I figure I need to race you through, and you need to keep your head down as much as possible. How about if we pretend you're someone I've picked up, and I've already got you three-quarters drunk before bringing you here to fleece you. That'd account for me not being there this afternoon, as well."

"This afternoon?"

She shrugged. "I was supposed to be dancing when I turned up at the offices, wasn't I?"

Bolan looked her up and down. As she walked with a sexy sway at his side, her skirt and top tight, he could imagine what she was like when undressed for work.

"Yeah, okay," he said finally. "Getting us into the club will be the hardest part. Once we're in there, we're on a level playing field. But while we're still outside, they have the territorial advantage."

They said no more until they reached the doorway that led down into the cellar-based club. There was only a short distance to cover, and in the evening heat of the city, Bolan felt a sweat begin under the heavy jacket. Looking around at the dress of the people around, he certainly felt that he, Stamp and Sugarman would look a little overdressed in the baggy jackets designed to hide the firearms they carried.

The streets were thronging with tourists and locals out for the evening, and the violence of the previous night hadn't acted in any way as a deterrent. Hopefully, Artruro had kept news of the violence in the club as quiet as possible, and so it would have escaped the notice of the police and the media, unlike the very public happenings at the rave club.

That was something that hadn't occurred to the soldier until this point—neither he, Stamp nor Sugarman had caught any news reports during the day. They had remained, in some ways, hermetically sealed in their own sphere of operations. What if the fight in the club had become public, and the club had been closed, or was under police surveillance?

He asked King quickly if she had heard anything.

Her reply came with a withering look. "I think I might have mentioned it to you if I had heard of anything, don't you? Besides, I phoned in earlier to try and sweet talk Artruro about missing my spot, and he couldn't come to the phone because he was busy with some little bit of business...another girl probably, from the way his goon told me about it. Probably thought I'd be really cut up to hear about it," she added savagely.

"As long as I know," he murmured. "Time to start acting."

They were almost level with the recessed doorway of the club when Bolan began to slump against King, forcing her to prop him upright. As he fell, and she steadied him, she could feel that this was no ordinary slump. Despite his apparent lack of balance, she could feel that every muscle was poised, and he knew exactly what he was doing.

She guided him into the doorway and down the stairs. The white walls and strip lighting on the staircase seemed to her to be directed solely at the man she was supporting, searching out his features for an identifying mark. She tried to dismiss this paranoia, but felt the muscles in her stomach tighten as they reached the foot of the stairs, and the lobby leading to the soundproofed door into the club. She also had to make a conscious effort not to glance nervously up to where she knew the security camera to be placed.

As for the Executioner's previous visit to the club, there was a receptionist seated at a table, ready to take admission fees and a security man in a black polo neck. It was the same blowsy blonde as the previous night, but the security man was different, the last incumbent of the post now resting peacefully in a landfill in the Essex countryside, courtesy of his boss's primitive methods of corpse disposal.

King and the soldier staggered into the lobby, Bolan keeping his head down. With the change in clothes, the added bulk beneath the jacket, and by keeping his face away from the woman as much as possible, he hoped he would pass unnoticed. The first words of the receptionist gave him hope.

"Jeez, Trace, where have you been? The old man's been going mental," she said, before adding in an undertone that was barely less raucous. "Who's your friend?"

"Never you mind, Sandy," King replied. "I've been spending the afternoon with this gentleman here, who now wants to see a genuine floor show. I told him I wouldn't be performing tonight, but we may have a little show later. He's certainly got enough on him to insure a good time," she added.

"Right, I see," the blonde said with a wink that the soldier caught from the corner of his eye as he stole a brief glance. She showed no sign of recognition, and seemed too gauche to be able to hide any such glimmers.

"You get the picture, then," King said heavily. "I'll just take him in myself, sort out the door money with you later, okay?"

"Okey-doke, sweetie."

King led the soldier forward toward the fire door. Then it happened. The soldier felt himself stayed by the hand of the security guard.

"Sorry, babe. Got to search him, just like the others," he said apologetically.

The soldier steeled himself. He could take the man by surprise with the Desert Eagle that nestled in his jacket pocket, and they could be through the door before the blonde could even scream.

But it wasn't necessary.

"Earl, leave them alone," the blonde said in a heavy whisper. "Don't piss the guy off before Trace has had a chance to...you know. Anyway," she added, "he's not going to be much trouble that pissed, is he?"

Bolan saw the man shrug and pull back.

"Thanks, Sandy, I owe you," King said as she pushed open the fire door.

Bolan knew they were in trouble without looking up.

The club was silent as the doors opened, and they were greeted by a heavily accented voice.

"Well, well, sweet thing. I wondered when you would show up. And such interesting company you're keeping these days, too."

12

Bolan looked up. The stage and table area was cleared, with nothing on the floor to get in the way of anyone should it come to a fight, which was looking a long shot, as there were eight men standing around the room, including Arturo, all evenly spaced apart to make any kind of shooting match little more than a spray-and-pray affair.

The soldier straightened, coming out of his act. There was little need for it now. He also recognized two of the eight—they were the Serbs he had encountered the previous afternoon at Heathrow. A resolve hardened in Bolan's heart. Even if he died, he would go down taking out those two bastards. That, after all, had been the original reason that had landed him here.

But his resolution was interrupted by the voice of the Maltese gang boss, who was taking the opportunity to swagger a little.

"So you're the asshole who took out some of my men and some of the Chinese right here last night, eh? And from what I hear, you and some other asshole took out a lot more later on. That—" he made a dismissive gesture "—that's their fuckup, and it don't bother me much. Just gives me a stick to beat them with if they get on my back, you know? But what you did here, that makes things a whole lot bad for me. And I don't like bad. I like things to be nice and easy. Shit, that's why I go into this business and not be a fuckin' cobbler like my father, or a road builder like my straight-ass brother."

He paused, allowing the others to laugh at a joke that he'd obviously made before. Then, when the brief burst of laughter had died down, his face grew dark as he continued.

"But you, you're worse even than that shit Arnie. He just double-cross and try to play both sides. He don't kill anyone and bring the police buzzing around here like flies on shit. You turn this quarter into the star attraction on *Murder Monthly* or something, bring all the spotlights and the filth and the press, all running around looking for something to give them a result, or to write about." He beat his chest as he continued, making Bolan feel he was a criminal who'd spent far too long watching gangster movies as a kid. "I work hard to pay off the right people and have a quiet life. I don't need some piece of shit like you making things difficult. And as for you—" he pointed a trembling finger at King "—just what's wrong with you, eh? What more could you possibly want from me? I give you a star spot, the chance to be by my side, and you turn against me. I ask you, boys," he said, turning to the assembled hoods, "what more could she possibly want?"

"My sister back."

King's voice had been low and insistent, and had cut through Sartini's bluster. In any other circumstances, Bolan would have found the confused expression on the face of the Maltese gang boss, and the comical double-take he affected when she spoke, almost laughable. But at this moment he cursed her interrupting Sartini's flow. For while the gang boss had been running off at the mouth, the moment of optimum surprise for the gangsters to take out the Executioner and the woman had passed. The men standing around the empty dance floor and auditorium were bored and twitchy. They knew of the soldier by reputation only of the previous evening, but it was enough for them to want to get the killing out of the way, before he had a chance to fight back. And their chief was so concerned at playing the godfather that he was prolonging the agony.

Good. The more strung-out their nerves got, then the easier they would be for the soldier to take. His survey had revealed that the Serbs were carrying identical MP-5s and Browning Hi-Powers. Two of the other mercenaries—possibly African—had a Colt Python .357 and an Uzi, and a Hi-Power and an MP-5 respectively. The remaining three gangsters were pale, thin men with dark hair and olive skin. They looked like younger versions of their boss, and were probably members of the same Maltese family business. One carried a sawed-off shotgun, the barrels tied together with silver wire; another carried a SIG-Sauer and a Smith & Wesson M-4000; and the last one had a CZ-75 semiautomatic and a P-38. Sartini himself carried a Colt Python .357 and a Glock, the only one Bolan had seen among the hardware carried by the gangsters, and obviously a long established personal favorite of the Maltese gang boss.

There was enough firepower there to reduce the Executioner and King to a bloody jelly of flesh and splintered bone, rendering them unrecognizable. Of that there was no doubt. But there was doubt about the men's reactions and their ability to snap into combat the longer their boss took to deliver the order.

And he had been suitably distracted from his oratory by King's comment.

The silence that followed made the gangsters look even more pained, more nervous. It was all the soldier could do to smile. With every second, the balance was tipping more and more toward an equilibrium. He was used to patience in a combat situation, and they weren't. Every passing second gave him back a little more ground.

"Your sister?" he said finally. "What the fuck are you talking about? Are you crazy or something?"

"My sister, who you sold down the line and sent off to be some piece of meat in a fucking brothel in the Far East," she said slowly, trying to keep her voice, and her temper, level.

"Sweetheart, I send a lot of girls off to carry drugs and be whores. How the fuck do you expect me to remember one from the other? Besides, it's only what I would have done to you eventually, when I got bored. Hey, anyway," he said with a sudden smile, "what the fuck does it matter to you, eh? What are you, the amount of times you swallowed my dick, eh?"

She sneered at him. "You know how many times I had to go and spew down the toilet after that?"

It was the perfect retort. Not only did it make him eye-poppingly angry, but Bolan could also see it broke the concentration of the three Maltese gangsters. Maybe it was a family joke, maybe not. Whatever, it made them have to work very hard not to laugh at their boss.

A better moment to act might never come.

Bolan took the Desert Eagle from his pocket, thumbing the safety and sighting and firing in one smooth motion. The .44 magnum shell left the barrel, rotating counterclockwise through the air to steady its line of flight. The intended target was one of the laughing Maltese gunmen. He barely had time to register surprise before the shell hit him in the lower chest. The spiraling bullet cut through the expensive silk shirt that he wore and pushed at his skin, for the merest moment drawing it tight from shoulder to groin as that very skin protested against the pressure and tried to withstand it to no avail. The skin split under the force and momentum of the shell, the flesh and layer of fat beneath the epidermis opening up before the soft-nosed shell with ease. It cut through the cross-hatched muscles over the ribs, and hit the bones themselves, its trajectory being disturbed for the first time by a firmer resistance.

Splinters of bone flew off his ribs, traveling at immense speed toward the heart, the lungs and down into the stomach and spleen. The damage caused by these secondary impacts would contribute more to the gunman's death than the slowed and skewed shell, which now made an exit wound that was larger through diffused force, and ripped through the now slack skin, tore at the silk shirt and shredded the fibers of the wool-mix suit jacket that the gangster wore over the expensive shirt. By the time that the shell was finishing its course, all power spent, embedding itself in the far wall, flattened into the plaster work and wallpaper, the gangster was already falling backward, thrown off his feet by the impact. He could still see, hear, and speak—or at least, would have screamed if the trauma had not paralyzed his cerebral cortex, the overload of sensation as he died frying his ability to respond. He was still dying as he thudded onto the floor, his body bouncing back up a few inches before coming to rest.

Before the shot had even achieved the first of these chain of events, Bolan was pushing King toward the bar area. He had half been expecting her to be paralyzed by shock at the sudden turn of events, the explosion of the Desert Eagle a deafening boom within the room, echoing around the empty walls. But the woman was made of sterner stuff than he had imagined, and the sudden thunder of the gun had galvanized her into action.

As the Serbs and the Africans swung their guns into firing positions, King pulled the CZ-75 semiautomatic from her shoulder bag and tapped the trigger twice, unleashing two shots at the Africans. One caught a gangster in the shoulder, making him drop his MP-5. He was still able to loose a couple of shots with the Hi-Power, the shells slamming into the optics above the bar, high above the woman's disappearing frame as she took the dive headfirst.

Bolan was a heartbeat behind, and that was enough for him to bring the Beretta to hand from its hiding place, a tap on the trigger drilling the wounded African from groin to neck, the gangster dancing a few steps back before falling to the ground. Even as he fired, the soldier executed a jackknife that took him over the surface of the bar, his knee catching the edge with a jarring jolt that ripped at his blue jeans. He stumbled as he landed, nearly colliding with King.

"Watch it!" she yelled above the roar of gunfire above their heads. "It's bad enough with them firing at me, without you at it, as well!"

Even as she spoke, she pulled the AKSU from her bag, leaving the CZ-75 by her side. In one fluid motion she snapped the collapsible stock into place, as Bolan had taught her only an hour or so before, and held the rifle above her head, the shortened barrel poking over the top of the bar. She tapped the trigger and fired in a wild arc, hoping that her spray and pray may just have an effect.

The screams from the other side were an encouragement, and she tapped another blast.

The soldier, meanwhile, had pulled one of Benny's rescued RGD-5 antipersonnel grenades from his pocket. He was aware that the bar behind which they were sheltering was lined with metal behind the wooden facade in order to prevent disgruntled customers kicking it in. However, the metal wouldn't be strong enough to hold back a firestorm if the gangsters on the other side suddenly lowered their arc of fire. At the moment, they were still reacting rather than acting, and were directing their fire at the area just cleared by the duo as they dived over the bar's surface. It didn't give Bolan much time in which to act, but perhaps enough.

He pulled the pin on the RGD-5, holding the spoon for a fraction of a second. Then, with a flip of his arm, he sent the fragmentation grenade sailing over the top of the bar and into what he judged would be the middle of the room. If his throw had been weighted correctly, it should hit and explode in the center of the raised dais area lined with poles.

"Keep down," he yelled, covering her body with his and hoping that the metal lining of the bar would be thick enough to withstand the shrapnel splinters of the grenade.

The floor of the room shook as the grenade detonated in the enclosed space. A rain of shrapnel hit the bar, splintering the wooden side, pitting and denting it, but thankfully not rupturing the metal skin that kept them shielded. The acoustic shock wave that hit the walls shook the last of the shattered optics from their holders, falling on the soldier as he kept King covered.

The gangsters' one mistake was that they had cleared the room of tables and chairs, anything that would provide them with cover from the grenade. The rain of metal following the detonation would have cut anyone within that enclosed space to ribbons.

"Heads up. Take out anything that's left standing," Bolan said to the woman, moving off her and into a crouch before coming upright behind the bar, ready to fire at anything that moved.

"Dammit," he cursed through teeth gritted in frustration. The door at the side of the bar was left swinging wide open, and it was obvious that the moment the grenade had flipped over the bar, the mobsters had considered discretion the better part of valour, and fled for the only exit.

Over by the soundproofed door leading to the lobby, the receptionist and the security man both lay in a mangled heap. It was evident that they had charged into the fray, armed with and MP-5 and an AKSU, which now lay near them, and had caught a full load of shrapnel at head level. Both their faces were recognizable.

The soldier hoped that the soundproofed door had swung shut behind them before the grenade had detonated. Just the reverberation along the cellars of all the buildings along the street would be suspicious enough, and the last thing he wanted was the blast to be heard from street level with so many police in the vicinity.

Besides these four corpses, there were two others, near the dais. The other Maltese gunmen hadn't been quick enough, unlike Artruro, the African, or the two Serbs. They had been hit in the back by the blast, the concussion alone being enough to kill them at that short distance by scrambling their internal organs.

That meant that four men had gotten away through the door into the back offices of the club: Sartini himself, one African and the two Serbs that Bolan wanted more than anything else.

"Come on, we've got to move quickly and carefully," he whispered to King, moving out from behind the bar. She didn't follow. The soldier turned and could see that she was frozen, not looking at the corpses but at the shattered and twisted remains of the poles that splayed out at obscene angles from the dais, the middle of which was just a blackened hole. It was as though she couldn't take in the bodies, but could comprehend the destruction of the area where she herself had once stood and gyrated.

"Traci," he said gently, touching her arm, reining in his impatience to begin the chase. He knew speed was of the essence, but they were still outnumbered two to one—he had no idea if there were other gunmen lurking in the back rooms—and he needed her to be alert and by his side, if only to maximize her own chance of survival.

She looked at him, for a moment seeming not to recognize who he was. Then the mist over her eyes cleared, and she focused again.

"Sorry, I was a bit shocked," she whispered.

"Let's go. They've moved into the back, and we've still got work to do."

They moved around the bar, taking the far side and coming through the now demolished trapdoor that had previously allowed the bar staff to pass behind and in front of the bar itself. This way, they could keep low and use what little shelter the remains of the bar provided as they attained the angle of the doorway leading to the back. The floor was slick with blood, and it was all King could do to keep her feet on the slippery floor. She paused to dispose of her shoes, preferring to risk her bare feet on the shrapnel covered floor.

"At least I can take a few splinters and ignore them—fat lot of good it'll do me to slip and fall when I should be shooting." She shrugged. Bolan marked it down as a point he'd overlooked in the need for speed. She should have worn running shoes or boots.

The layout of the back rooms in the cellar came to mind. He tried to remember all that he had seen and been told when the blueprints had been uncovered in the A-rave-daze office. The additional rooms housed offices, rest rooms for the hired hands when they were on duty but not actually going about their business and the strong room in which Sartini housed his takings, drugs and extra cash. As far as he could recall, there had been no exit marked on the plans other than through the lobby and the staircase to the street; considering how many planning restrictions this broke for the legitimate business, he could easily see how much money had changed hands in bribes. What it did, however, was make the cellar a defensive fortress, with only the one seeming exit and entrance. No others.

But no one got to Sartini's position without a little forward planning. The exit wouldn't even be in the blueprints. It would be a little something off paper. The old sewers in the city center of London ran close to the surface, as did the crisscrossing old rivers on which the city had been built, all feeding into the Thames and all long-ago pushed underground. But they were there; and they were the escape route.

Bolan knew that he had to move fast, before Sartini had a chance to access that escape route.

The open door at the side of the bar led down a corridor lit by two low-wattage bulbs, one at each end. The lighting may have been low, but it was still brighter than the club room, where all the lighting overhead had been blown out by the frag grenade. The only illumination in the larger room was that thrown out of the doorway: this gave Bolan and his companion the advantage of being hidden from view, and meant that anything the opposition gunmen did by way of entering the corridor could be clearly seen; they would present nicely lighted targets.

But it also meant that as soon as Bolan crossed that threshold, until he or the woman could find cover, then they, too, were easy meat.

The soldier hunkered down at the angle of the bar, scanning the territory ahead. King crouched at his shoulder. Three doors led off the corridor, which extended back for about fifteen feet: two on their left, and one on the right. As the corridor wasn't that deep, it suggested the rooms were either not that big, or extended back in a rectangular rather than square shape. One of them had to be the strong room, one the mob boss's office and one the restroom. He couldn't say for sure, but if he remembered the blueprints correctly, and the design followed logic, then it was probable that the single door to the right was the strong room. It was equally likely that any escape route wouldn't be through there. King knew the club and could tell him. He asked her quickly.

"Us artistes changed in a room off the lobby, and when I had to keep Artie entertained, it was at his apartment. Dancers and bar staff didn't go back there," she whispered.

Okay, time to think again.

All three doors were closed, and the corridor was deathly silent. The onus was on the Executioner to move, as time was of the essence. Sartini and his men could either wait it out, or they could use the escape route. But Bolan and King had a further appointment with death, so this operation had to be mopped up, and quickly.

The door on the right was closed. The two doors on the left appeared to be closed, but it was possible that they were open a fraction, someone watching for signs of movement.

As soon as he or King set foot into the corridor, either of those doors could open, and a hail of lead could greet them.

Bolan looked at the ceiling of the corridor, which looked to be plasterboard and paper, painted over. But underneath that? Just to have the club down here would mean that the cellar had been excavated onto the foundations of the old building. In order for the builder to do that and then support the weight of the old buildings up above, there had to have been some severe reinforcement of the joists and flooring underpinning the old houses.

Which meant—he hoped—that the enclosed corridor would just collapse around their ears and cut off the side rooms if he carried out what seemed to be the sole option. Firstly because he wanted to get at the four—perhaps more—gunmen left in one or both of those rooms, and secondly because he had a feeling that if they were going to evade the police and make it to their rendezvous with Sugarman and Stamp, they might have to find and avail themselves of the emergency exit he was sure Sartini had hidden away.

Bolan had already used the RGD-5s he had been carrying, but King had more with her. Bolan took two of the grenades from her shoulder bag.

"Get back behind the bar, brace yourself and be ready to move when I say—and to shoot anything that moves," he whispered to her. Her brown eyes wide with fear and an adrenaline buzz, pupils large in the darkness, she nodded and turned her back to the bar, opening her mouth to equalize the pressure when the grenades detonated. It was something that Bolan had been adamant about when running through the weaponry, and after the previous explosion she wasn't about to make the mistake of forgetting it this time.

The Executioner pulled the pin on the first grenade, let the spoon fly and rolled the bomb along the corridor until it hit the end wall. Even while it was in motion, he took the pin from the second, freed the spoon and rolled the orb with less momentum, so it stopped almost in front of the door nearest the entrance to the club room. He then flung himself back around the bar, back braced, mouth open.

The explosions followed so rapidly on top of each other that they sounded like one slightly extended blast. The room rocked, and clouds of dust from plaster and brick billowed out into the club room. It also went momentarily dark, as the lights in the corridor were blown, the bulbs shattered and the socket blasted out of the ceiling as the plasterboard was shredded by the grenades.

The glimmers of light that did creep out after the billowing clouds showed that the side rooms were on different circuits, and that their doors had been blown in by the blast—which was exactly what the soldier had wanted. The question was, how much rubble was now strewed in their path as they hit the rooms to mop up the opposition?

Only one way to find out.

"Go!" Bolan yelled, coming upright and moving around the bar, the SWA-12 assault shotgun now his main weapon of choice. The shot from the heavy-duty assault gun would be the quickest way to spread mayhem in the enclosed rooms.

King was on his heels, the AKSU cradled in her arms. She followed Bolan toward the light, motes of still settling dust swirling in the beam as they negotiated the carnage caused by the grenades.

The doorway to the corridor was no longer there, as such. Instead, it had been enlarged to an uneven, jagged hole in the wall. Brick and plaster was strewed out into the club room, and in the dim illumination, Bolan could see that the entire ceiling of the corridor had collapsed, plasterboard, brick and sparking wiring hanging down to litter the floor. The doors to the two rooms on the left had also vanished, blown inward by the blast. The doorways here were also enlarged, chunks of plaster and brick having been blown out, the walls on either side showing damage where the shrapnel had taken out chunks of the plaster. Interestingly, the door on the right had remained relatively untouched. It showed superficial fragmentation damage, but was otherwise intact.

Definitely the strong room. So all attention should be focused on the rooms on the left.

Bolan and King were over the bricks, the soldier leaping across the chasm caused by the blast, playing the odds that whoever was inside was too stunned by the blast to have the reactions to fire as he passed. He and King were backs to the wall on each side of the door. He looked across and nodded to her.

As they turned into the doorway, King tapped the trigger of the AKSU, spraying the room with fire. Bolan let loose two blasts from the SWA-12, the booms of the shotgun seeming strangely quiet after the magnitude of the blasts.

There was no answering fire.

The Executioner gestured for her to stay and moved crablike along the wall until he was close to the farthest doorway. He then counted three, turned and sprayed the interior of the room with fire from the SWA-12 before flattening himself once more against the wall.

There was silence, somehow more deafening than the fire that had preceded it. He gestured to King to enter the room, while he entered the farthest one. Another gesture indicated that she should use extreme caution, despite the lack of returned fire. She spared him a grin that questioned, Do I look that stupid?

Bolan stepped into the far room. It went back for fifteen feet, and the far end was damaged only by the blasts of the SWA-12 fire. It had been the rest room for the enforcers, and there were tables and easy chairs, a now shattered TV and video and a bar that was leaking spirits onto the dust-covered carpet.

But there was no sign of any life—nor any corpses.

"Mike, in here," King called.

At the double, Bolan left the room and made his way to the office, where the woman was waiting. It was a smaller room, with less depth. The office furniture and the computer terminal were now little more than matchwood, the bar nothing more than a stain on the dust- and plaster-covered carpet, which was also stained red with blood.

Blood that was seeping from the African, a ragged, raw wound where his chest should have been, and one of the Serbs. Which one Bolan couldn't tell, as either the blast from the grenades or a blast from the AKSU or SWA-12 had taken his face away.

The soldier looked down at him. Fifty percent of the debt for Heathrow—the woman from the concession stand, the father of the boy and girl, and the others—was settled.

But the other Serb was still at bay. So was Sartini.

"The other two in there?" King asked, indicating the other room with an inclination of her head. And when Bolan shook his in reply, she asked, astonished, "Where have they gone, then?"

"Good question. There must be a bolt-hole out of here."

Without hesitation, the soldier moved across the room. It had to be at the far end of the room away from the door; otherwise they would have seen it. He moved behind the remains of Sartini's desk and found what he was looking for. The carpet had been pulled back, and a manhole cover had been shifted onto the floor. An old, rusting ladder led down into darkness. Bolan guessed that this manhole into the sewers had been here since the buildings above had been originally erected, and that its location was the reason that Sartini had taken this room as his office.

It would be dark down there, and quiet. The two gangsters didn't have much of a head start, and King and himself should be able to track them relatively easily.

Bolan turned to tell her the plan of action, only to be taken up short by the sight of her pulling the running shoes off the feet of the dead Serb.

"What—" he began.

"Just give me a second," she said without looking up. "My feet are going to really suffer if I don't get some shoes, and I'd be no good to you then." She pulled the left, then the right shoe and put them on her own feet. "You know, he's got little feet for such a big bloke, but then I've got big feet for a girl...and I've never been so glad of it as now. They're a bit loose, but not so's they'd fall off. Now, where has that shitbag Artie gone?"

Despite the tension of the situation, Bolan had to resist the temptation to grin at the coolness of the woman. She was now on her feet, AKSU cradled, and ready to continue. The soldier explained briefly what he suspected, and she nodded.

"Let's do it, then," she said simply.

Bolan led the way down the manhole tunnel, feeling carefully for the rusted rungs of the ladder with his feet. When nothing but air hung beneath the final rung, he lowered himself carefully. His toes touched a slimy stone surface, and he allowed himself to drop down, landing softly. He told King about the extent of the drop and caught her about the waist as she lowered herself. She was hot, sweating, and she felt good against him as she let herself drop.

As their eyes adjusted to the gloom, they could see that there was a dim illumination in the tunnel, from phosphorescent paint used to coat the walls, and from some light sources accessing from the streets above, filtering down through the drains in the curbs. The smell was almost overpowering, and it took some effort not to heave at the stench. Listening, they could hear the splashing of two sets of feet, running to their left.

Why were they running in the shallow water rather than on the stone walkway at the side?

Bolan tried the stone with his feet. It was slippery, covered in moss and slime.

"Think you can keep your balance on it?" he asked King.

"Only one way to find out." She shrugged. "It'd be quieter—they wouldn't hear us...."

Bolan nodded, then set off at a jog after the retreating sounds of splashing feet. As he moved, he became surer footed, and increased his pace. He could hear King at his heels, increasing her own pace.

At this rate, they would soon catch up with Sartini and the Serb, whose own progress was actually being impeded by their choice to run in the water. Bad choice for them, good choice for the Executioner.

The tunnels curved, with smaller tunnels running off them. At one end, they terminated in the Thames, but at the other? A way out, and this was where Sartini and the Serb were headed.

The splashing was louder now. They weren't much farther ahead.

"Try and keep the Maltese alive. The other one's mine," Bolan whispered as they ran. He had the Beretta and the Desert Eagle in his hands, while King carried the AKSU. They were staying cautious and alert. The nearer they got, the greater the chance of their own footsteps being heard in the cavernous echo of the tunnel.

"Wait—back," Bolan yelled suddenly, throwing out an arm to catch the woman and take her with him as he flattened to the tunnel wall. The rapid-fire boom of an MP-5 echoed around them as splinters of stone flew out of the wall a few feet beyond where they stood. It was followed by the hollow explosion of a Glock.

Bolan turned and tapped the Beretta's trigger, arcing a 3-round burst at the bend in the tunnel. It was enough to stop the firing, but their two assailants were still out of view. "Cover me," he said quickly, splashed across the sewer floor as King let fly with a covering arc of AKSU fire. He kept low, avoiding the sporadic return fire as their opponents took cover of their own.

He made the far side of the tunnel and flattened himself to the wall. From there he had a good view of both men, who had lost sight of him in the darkness. He could see their faces, frantically scanning the walls to find him.

He wasn't about to give them the chance. Leveling the Desert Eagle, Bolan targeted Sartini first. One shot, and the Maltese gang boss was sent spinning as the Glock flew from his hand, rendered useless by the .44 Magnum slug that ripped open his upper arm.

The Serb brought round the MP-5, sighting Bolan. He was sharp and quick, but the Executioner was quicker.

Even as the first shot echoed in the tunnel, the soldier squeezed the trigger for a second. The rounds ran straight and true, drilling holes in the Serb's forehead and slamming him back against the wall. The exit wounds spread his skull and brain matter across the phosphorescent brick. He slumped down the wall.

One hundred percent retribution.

Now for the other matter. Bolan moved across toward Sartini, who was almost crying in agony at the wound in his arm. The soldier heard King's footsteps on the stone as she raced to join them.

"Damn, that was a class act," she breathed. "But why do we want the bastard alive?" she added, prodding the sobbing Sartini with the muzzle of the AKSU.

"Because we've still got another appointment to make," Bolan replied with a humorless grin.

One she returned as she realized his meaning.

13

Sugarman and Stamp had lingered a long time over the one drink, and the big man was starting to clock-watch with an increasing frequency. His cell phone lay on the table between them, beside the almost empty glasses.

"You reckon anything's gone wrong, Dan?" he asked in quiet, reflective tones as he looked at the phone and then up at the clock on the wall behind his partner's head.

Sugarman shrugged. He'd been looking almost constantly out the window at the restaurant across the main road, and was developing a kink in his neck.

"I don't," he said finally. "But it's getting to the point where we need to do something. I'm getting too tense with all this, and I won't be able to do anything before long."

"Yeah, I know," Stamp murmured, flexing his aching

shoulder. "If this gets any stiffer, I won't be much use to anyone, either."

The phone rang suddenly, seeming to cut through the hubbub of noise on the bar.

Both men stared at the phone, momentarily mesmerized, unable to pick it up.

"So are you going to answer it, or what?" Sugarman asked, staring hard at the phone and unable to pick it up for himself.

"Yeah, sure," Stamp said, visibly shaking himself out of a trance to reach out for the cell phone. "Tell you what," he added, "it better not be Steph checking up on where you are. I can't answer for what I might say if it is...."

But as soon as the big man heard the voice on the other end, Sugarman could see from his face that it was the soldier. A few words, with Stamp merely saying "Okay" at the end before slipping the phone into his pocket. The tension was almost too much for the detective.

"Well?" he asked impatiently.

Stamp drowned the last of his beer and put the glass back on the table. His face was stone, his eyes glittering.

"We've got a go, Dan. Belasko and Traci are on their way, and they've got Uncle Artie with them."

"Shit," Sugarman whispered. In truth, his anxieties told him that this wasn't, perhaps, what part of him wanted to hear.

But the showdown was, ultimately, inevitable.

The two men sat in silence for a couple of seconds. Sugarman was the first to move.

"Let's do it," he said softly to his partner.

"DO YOU KNOW where we are? And I mean exactly," the soldier said sharply to Sartini as he finished bandaging the wound to the man's arm. He had managed to staunch the flow of blood and bind the wound so that they could pass among the crowds above without too much notice.

Too much notice? Who was he kidding? They were, all three of them, wet from head to foot, and had to have smelled and looked appalling. A person couldn't be involved in a running chase through a main sewer without suffering the consequences. In order to avoid suspicion, and attract as little attention as possible from the public and—particularly—from the police who were in the area, they had to be aboveground for as little time as possible.

Being underground in the sewer system could be used to their advantage. They could move unimpeded until they were within a short distance of the restaurant, then come aboveground and hit it. It was the perfect plan—provided they knew exactly where they were. And, as Bolan was no expert on the sewer tunnels of central London, he had to rely on the Maltese gang boss. Sartini had the manhole in his office as an escape route; therefore he had to know where he could break ground again.

And time was of the essence. Not only did Bolan want to hit the restaurant before news of the assault on the lap-dancing club reached triad ears, but he also knew that it was only a matter of time before the police were hot on their trail. There had been enough explosions to attract attention from the street, and enough gunfire in the tunnels to drift up to the street through the drainage system. Even if this was lost on street level because of traffic noise, as soon as the law-enforcement agencies found the carnage in the club, they'd find the opened manhole in the office and be flooding the tunnels with armed men.

Sartini was being no help at the moment. The Maltese was in shock from the wound.

"Pull yourself together and answer me, Sartini. Do you know exactly where we are?"

Sartini shook his head, gasping through his tears. "How the fuck am I supposed to know? I lost it when you chased us. You prick, you think they let you get away with this?"

"Who, the Chinese?" Bolan asked. And when Sartini nodded, the soldier added, "Well, we'll soon find out, won't we?"

He stepped back and looked up and down the tunnel. If Sartini either couldn't or wouldn't give him a location, he was going to have to find out for himself. And there was only one way to do this.

"Keep a close watch on him. Don't let the bastard even breathe unless you give him permission," Bolan instructed King.

"It'll be a pleasure," she said flatly. "What are you going to do?"

"Try and find out where the hell we are," Bolan told her, setting off in the direction they had originally come from. If he remembered correctly...

Yes. Just past the bend, and the wall peppered with MP-5 fire, was a metal ladder, rusted like the one they had used, leading up into a cutting made through the roof of the sewer tunnel. It had to terminate in another manhole. And the soldier thought it unlikely it would be in a cellar or building of any kind, as adjacent to the ladder was an inlet leading up the street, admitting some light and sound.

Pocketing the Beretta and the Desert Eagle, Bolan jumped up and grabbed hold of the bottom rung of the ladder, pulling himself up hand-over-hand until he was able to get a foothold on the ladder, which was swaying precariously, protesting with a loud creak as it took the soldier's weight. He moved up the ladder swiftly, narrowing his shoulders to fit into the enclosed space of the tunnel.

The manhole was definitely at street level. He could tell by the depth of the narrow brick enclave, which felt as though it were closing in around him, the dank brick almost touching his face as he climbed. It was a good job that he wasn't claustrophobic; besides, there were other things to worry about. For all he knew, the manhole could come up in the middle of the road, and any attempt to move it could see him decapitated by a passing vehicle. Or there could be a vehicle parked or standing over the manhole cover, making it impossible to move. Or even just someone standing on it, their weight enough to hold the cover in place when there was no room for the soldier to maneuver his shoulders in the narrow tunnel, no way for him to gain purchase.

As it was, it proved difficult to actually move his arms into a position where he could bend and flex his elbows to lever the cover upward, the tunnel shaft being so narrow that he could only raise his arm straight, as they had been for clasping the rungs of the ladder.

The sweat gathered on his forehead, running into his eyes and stinging as he pushed. With little leverage, every muscle in his upper and lower arms was strained, the power of his torso proving of no use in this position. He gritted his teeth and ignored the soreness in his eyes. Gradually, the cover lifted enough for him to be able to push the lip over the rim and balance it on the roadway above. He blinked as the sudden daylight assaulted his already sore eyes, and pushed the cover far enough over for him to be able to put his head up into the fresh air. But first he listened—the traffic noises were fairly distant, suggesting that this was a side road.

Carefully—ready to pull in at any moment should traffic be headed his way—Bolan looked up and over the rim of the manhole.

A curious passerby was watching. Bolan gave the man a smile and said, "Routine check, sir..."

The passerby shrugged and continued his walk. In a way, Bolan would have liked to have asked the man where he was, but that could invite too many questions he didn't have the time to answer, nor did he want a suspicious pedestrian searching out a police officer.

He looked up and down the street. He was near enough to one end to see the road name on the wall of an old building— Meard Street. He was familiar with the name and knew whereabouts it was in Soho. One end was near Dean Street, while the other ended in a dead end with Wardour Street running parallel to Dean, but cut off by the back of an office building.

Okay. Now that he knew where he was, he had the compass points, and knew the direction in which the sewer ran. He popped back down into the shaft, pulling the cover back into place behind him. He scrambled down the ladder and dropped onto the sewer floor, keeping the compass points in mind. As he traced the tunnel back to where King was waiting with Sartini, he compared it to the mental map of the streets overhead, and worked out that they were heading in the right direction for the restaurant, and all they needed to do was keep on until they found the nearest point of exit.

As he rounded the corner, he found the woman holding the AKSU to Sartini's head. The wounded mob boss was sitting on the stone path, back to the tunnel wall, sobbing softly. King was talking to him in a quiet voice that only became intelligible as Bolan drew near.

"...lucky bastard, really. Otherwise I'd kill you slowly right now, starting by blowing your balls off. Bet you'd want to tell me what happened to Elena then, wouldn't you? Only it'd be in a really high-pitched voice. Tell you what, I want you alive as long as possible, maybe let those triad guys blow your balls off for selling them out before we wipe the floor with them."

"Take it easy," Bolan said quietly as he drew near.

King turned and looked at the soldier with disbelief. "Easy?"

"Yeah. We want him still functioning for now. He's got to get us into the restaurant. Last thing we need is for him to break down on the street and attract too much attention before we're in."

The woman's nostrils flared as she breathed hard, trying to control her temper. "Yeah, you're right, dammit," she said slowly. "So, any idea where we are?"

"Yeah—and guess what? He's got us halfway there already. So let's get going."

"You heard the man, scumbag," King said, prodding Sartini with the muzzle of the AKSU. "On your feet and start moving."

The mob boss scrambled to his feet and walked on in front of Bolan and the woman, sobbing to himself and babbling in a mixture of Maltese and English. He figured his time on this earth was limited, and seemed to be trying to make his peace with God.

"Traci, keep him covered, and wait for me."

Bolan had figured out that they were within a couple of streets of the restaurant, and if he was really lucky, then this shaft would take them up into the alleyway in which he had first seen the triad gunners on the previous afternoon. He sure as hell hoped so; he didn't like the idea of coming up into the thoroughfare and having his head taken off by a passing truck or car.

He knew he had to move quickly, now. Once he had the manhole cover removed, it would only be a matter of a short time before it attracted the attention of the police. So they had to be out of the shaft and away in an optimum time.

He ascended the ladder as swiftly as possible and braced his elbows against the slimy brickwork to lift the manhole cover, hoping the cover would be free from obstruction.

The manhole cover gave gracefully, and he was able to lever it out of position, heaving it clear of the hole. He listened, but all seemed quiet. Popping his head over the rim, he could see that his calculations had been correct, and they had arrived at the alleyway. At the end, he could see the crowds on the main drag, and the restaurant.

Shinning down the ladder until his foot was on the bottom rung, he looked down and could just see King and Sartini.

"We're going to have move quickly. Sartini, when I drop down, grab my legs and let me pull you up to the ladder. Then you follow me, and quickly. If you don't, she can shoot you right here." He paused for a second and could hear the fear in the mob boss's voice as he agreed in a monosyllable.

Bolan continued, "You follow, Traci. I think you can make the distance to the bottom rung."

"Sweetie, there isn't much you can teach me about poles and leaping about, is there?"

Bolan paused, recalling the athletic pole dancer he had seen previous evening on his first visit to the club. Yeah, maybe she would have no problem.

"Okay, let's do it," he said, dropping down.

He felt the pull of the mob boss's almost deadweight on

his legs, and he began to haul himself upward, muscles straining at the extra weight, the rungs on the rusted ladder protesting at the extra weight in a similar manner. He hoped they would hold until Sartini got a hold.

Fear can be an incredible thing. For a man with such a wound, Sartini showed incredible strength and determination in grabbing the rungs and hoisting himself up the shaft in the wake of the soldier. Despite the pain, he moved like a man fitter and younger than his years. Bolan was out on the street and lifting the mob boss clear before he knew it.

Down on the sewer tunnel floor, King watched them go. She folded the stock of the AKSU and slipped it into her shoulder bag, which she opened and repositioned, one strap on each shoulder, like a rucksack, so that it was in the middle of her back and no longer an imbalance.

She judged the distance and braced herself. One of the reasons she had been able to pass as a pole dancer with ease was that she had been a gymnast as a child, and several weeks of gym work had soon regained her strength and suppleness she had never entirely lost.

She would need it now. From a standing jump, she made it as far as the bottom rung, which brushed against her fingertips. Not enough to get a firm grip. She fell down with a gasp.

But at least she had the distance gauged. Taking a few deep breaths, she stepped back enough to make a running jump. As she leaped, she felt herself grab hold of the bottom rung, clinging on while she swung wildly, her momentum almost breaking the grip. She flung hand over hand, still swinging as she climbed, wincing and swearing as her shoulder and elbows crashed painfully against the stone. Gradually, she made her way up until she was able to put one foot on the bottom rung. That steadied the swaying, and she was then able to scale the ladder quickly, coming up blinking into the daylight, hands on the asphalt to push herself free of the shaft.

"Anything's going to be easy after that," she gasped, coming to her feet and pushing the manhole cover back into place before taking the bag off her shoulders and adjusting it to a more conventional carrying style.

While she did that, Bolan had his eye on Sartini, who was seated on the curb, seemingly exhausted. The soldier didn't trust him, and had the Desert Eagle in his hand, barely concealed beneath the jacket.

Once King had the manhole cover in place, Bolan took out the cell phone, pressed Memory, found Sugarman's number and punched Dial.

It rang a few times before Stamp answered.

"Belasko," Bolan said shortly. "We have Sartini. We're in the alley opposite the front of Hoo Hing. We're moving now. Keep us under observation and follow at a discreet distance. See you on the other side of this, guys."

He turned off the phone and slipped it into his pocket.

"Ready?" he asked King. When she nodded, he prodded Sartini with his toe. "Move it. And remember we're on your back every step of the way. Cross the street and go straight in. They'll be surprised to see you...especially like this."

14

"Will you look at that," Sugarman breathed to his partner as they hit the sidewalk.

"Tell me I'm not really seeing it," the big man answered. "Tell me I'm not, Dan...."

Sugarman shook his head slowly, an indulgent grin spreading across his face. "I can tell you, Justin, my old son, but I'd be lying. You're seeing it, all right."

The two private detectives stood outside the bar, watching as Bolan and King weaved through the busy traffic, Arturo Sartini preceding them, the Maltese gangster so disheartened that he didn't even bother to respond to the insults of the drivers whose way he barred, preferring instead to keep his eyes fixed to the ground.

All three of them looked filthy, their clothes ripped and torn, covered in mud and scum from the sewer. Stamp wasn't sure, but it felt as though he could smell them from where he stood. One thing was for sure—considering that Belasko hadn't wanted to be conspicuous, he seemed to have gone out of his way to achieve the opposite effect. Even in the middle of a Soho night, with the strangeness and eccentricity that fueled the area of excess, the trio still stood out.

"Never mind hanging back, Dan. We'd better stick close to them," he muttered to his colleague. "The Chinese will suss them out straight away, and it's not going to take long to reach the ears of the cops, especially after the last day or so."

Sugarman agreed. "I'm with you on that. They're going to need backup."

The two men waited until the trio preceding them had entered the restaurant by the revolving door, then set off across the street, taking care not to stop the traffic and draw attention to themselves.

Bolan, King and Sartini had vanished from view by the time they reached the far sidewalk and the revolving door.

THE EXECUTIONER WAS aware of the stares that he and the two people with him were attracting as they passed through the swing door of the restaurant and entered the lobby. It was small and crowded, with people jamming the double doors into the ground-floor dining area, and the staircases that wound up on either side, taking those in search of sustenance to the dining areas on the other floors.

He was also aware that their passage across the road had attracted no little attention. That would mean that Lin Ho and his men knew they were coming, and it would mean that a suspicious police force, alert for anything unusual in an area that had suddenly become a war zone, would be checking out reports. Either way, things were closing in, and they didn't have much time.

Sartini paused in the lobby and looked back over his shoulder at the two people behind him. Bolan had the Desert Eagle barely concealed beneath the loose jacket, his other hand free, fingers flexing occasionally, ready to grab another weapon at the first sign of attack. King had one hand on her shoulder bag, holding it across her midriff. Her other was in the bag, fingers closed comfortingly around the stock of the CZ-75. As the gang boss's eyes met his captors', Bolan could see there was complete defeat in them. Sartini was tired, in pain, and his ashen face showed that it was taking all his willpower to stay upright. Wherever a problem arose, it wouldn't come from him.

"What do you want now?" the Maltese asked.

"Lin Ho—where do you meet him?"

"Usually third floor."

"Yeah, but where?"

"In the restaurant itself. He keeps a table near the window facing the street. That way he can see out while he's doing business." The ghost of a malevolent smile flickered across the Maltese gang boss's lips.

Bolan cursed to himself. The triad chief would have seen them cross the road, heard the protesting traffic. He'd be ready. The question was, what would he do about it?

"Then we go up," the soldier said flatly. "I assume you know the way."

Sartini shrugged and headed for the staircase. In his heart, he knew that he was a dead man either way. If these two didn't ice him, then Lin Ho would for screwing up so badly. His only consolation was that he might be able to take these bastards with him.

But something unusual was going on. The stairwells were even more crowded than usual, and it was mostly with a downtide of people. Those trying to ascend had to really push their way through a muttering throng. Bolan thought he caught some disgruntled conversation from some of the passersby about the third floor being suddenly closed down, even those already in their seats being evicted by the officious waiters.

So Lin Ho was ready for them.

When Sartini reached the third floor, he turned to find the way barred by a group of Chinese waiters, who were evicting the last straggling diners and turning away those who wished to enter. One of them put up a hand to bar his way, dropping it suddenly when another Chinese almost imperceptibly shook his head. The waiter wrinkled his nose in disgust as the sewage-covered Maltese passed by and entered the dining room, before having to devote his attention to an irate diner who suddenly wanted to know why the three new arrivals could enter the third floor, and not him and his friends.

King and Bolan were close behind.

"Get ready—it's a trap," Bolan whispered to her. She nodded, and he could see the sparkle of adrenaline-drenched fear in her eyes.

The waiters—whose clothes bore the telltale line of concealed weapons to Bolan's trained eye—let them pass, and they cautiously entered the third-floor dining room, where Sartini stood in the middle, looking around with an expression suggesting that he felt a little lost.

There was a table by the window, and Bolan could see five men seated—four were enforcers, one of whom he was sure he had encountered once before. But the fifth man he knew instantly: Lin Ho. The Chinese had cold, glittering eyes that appraised them, and a thin moustache that accentuated the hard set of his mouth. He was older than Bolan remembered, but had not run to fat—rather, his face had grown lined, like a weathered tree. Hard, like teak.

The rest of the room appeared to be empty, the tables still covered with the remains of meals that had been interrupted midway. There were no other Chinese in view. The only ones that Bolan was aware of were those behind, and they still seemed to be occupied by the rush of irate customers.

Could Lin Ho really want a firefight here, in the middle of Soho, in his restaurant, betraying his base of operations?

"Keep your eye on them," Bolan ordered King, suddenly whirling as his almost sixth sense for danger, honed over many years of combat, kicked in, warning him of trouble.

As the soldier turned, bringing the Desert Eagle up from beneath his jacket, he saw that two of the waiters on the outside were pulling closed the doors to the dining room.

Turning back, he could see that King had dropped the bag to her side and had the CZ-75 in her hand.

The five men around the table were still sitting calmly, apparently unarmed. Finally, Lin Ho spoke. His voice was clear, his English barely accented, with just the faintest of London twangs.

"So you're the gentleman—or one of them—who has been causing so much trouble. And a woman, too. I congratulate you as a warrior of the gentler sex."

"That's big of you," King snapped.

Lin Ho allowed himself a grimace that may possibly have been a twisted smile. "It is, though I do not expect you to appreciate that fact. You have given us a lot of trouble in such a short time, and now we are face to face, I believe that we may have crossed paths once before."

"Perhaps...a long time ago," Bolan said calmly.

Lin Ho nodded. "I suspect as much. And you were a problem then, as now. But, I fear, you would not have become a problem if not for the bungling incompetents that this fool chooses to employ," he added, inclining his head toward Sartini. "If not for the clowns that he sent to the airport, you would have been on your way to wherever you were headed, to whatever you had to do, without causing us the slightest pain or grief."

Bolan shrugged. "Bad day for you."

"Or for our incompetent associate, here," Lin Ho qualified. "I am now giving you a fair warning. I will reach slowly into my pocket and withdraw a pistol. It will not be aimed at you."

With which, the Chinese warlord began, with painstaking slowness, to reach into his jacket.

"Mike—" King began.

"Slowly, Lin Ho."

Lin Ho withdrew a Browning Hi-Power from his shoulder holster, and without a word leveled the pistol and drilled the Maltese gang boss in the head. Sartini was looking toward Bolan and King when the shot was fired, and it entered at the back of his skull, exiting through his right eye. Brain and blood spray spewed from him as his twisting body corkscrewed to the floor.

In one quiet move Lin Ho leveled the Browning toward the Executioner.

"And so we have a stalemate, I believe. I have no wish to kill you here, where it could cause so much trouble. But I will, if you resist. You cannot kill us all, and you will be taken and kept alive. So it would perhaps be best for you to surrender now, and perhaps save yourself some pain...and the girl, of course," he added, before barking something in Cantonese.

Bolan and King both whirled instinctively as the two single doors to the kitchen were kicked open. Two waiters and two cooks, holding MP-5s, spilled into the room. When the soldier looked back, the four enforcers around Lin Ho were on their feet, holding Colt Pythons and P-38s.

"Mike—" King began again.

"It's okay," Bolan reassured her. "We'd be dead meat now if they didn't want us alive, and I'm kind of curious to find out why."

He was also curious as to how long it would take Sugarman and Stamp to arrive. Curious to find out if they would attack. Curious to find out if Lin Ho's men were aware of their presence...

"WHERE THE HELL are they all going?" Sugarman shouted to his partner over the noise made by the crowd.

"I don't know, but they seem to have come from the third, so that must be where the action is," the big man replied, having overheard some of the exchanges on the stairs as they climbed against the tide.

"Where have Belasko and Traci got to?" Sugarman asked, feeling frustrated at being able to do nothing except mouth questions. But before he could elicit an answer from Stamp, the sound of a single shot was heard above the voices of the crowd, voices that were suddenly raised in anger and confusion as panic began to set in.

Without a word, both men began to push harder against the crowd, fighting their way through to reach the third floor.

That had to be where the action was, a supposition supported by the closed doors and the waiters outside.

"Does that tell you anything, Dan?" the big man asked. "And I'll tell you what else—I bet they're carrying more than menu cards," he added as he saw the waiters lined up outside the doors. Some of them were reaching into their white linen jackets. "We've been made, Dan. It's time to rock and roll," he yelled, pulling the M-4000 from beneath his jacket.

"IT STRIKES ME that a man of your talents and stature—one who has stayed alive for so long in an atmosphere that is so hostile—wouldn't come amongst us unless for a reason. And I intend to find that reason. For that alone, you shall not die yet. You may rest assured that, if you tell us all, then you will die quickly."

Bolan grinned without humor. "And you really think that such a considerate assumption is going to make me talk— even assuming there's anything to say."

"Oh, there must be something to say. This can't be mere coincidence. And if you won't talk for your own sake, then you will talk for that of the woman."

Bolan didn't dare to look at King. The fact that she was in this situation was down to him. He could have refused her taking part, but there was nothing more to this battle than the coincidence that Lin Ho would disdain. How the hell could he spare her torture when he had nothing to say? Not that he trusted the Chinese warlord's word. He needed action, and he needed it now. There were nine Chinese in the room, against himself and the woman. And no cover. They had conquered similar odds at the lap-dancing club, but the enemy had been inferior to these trained triad gunners.

The soldier badly needed a break.

That's when he heard the boom of the M-4000, and the splintering of the dining-room doors.

STAMP STOOD HIS GROUND, the recoil on the Smith & Wesson shotgun driving back into his wounded shoulder, the kick making him roar with agony. It was a good feeling, which made him mean, spurred him on. Shifting the barrel of the shotgun a few inches to the right, he let fly with another charge, this time better prepared for the kick of the recoil.

The first charge had flown into the main group of waiters grouped by the closed doors, hitting them at chest and abdomen level. The shot was fast and furious at such close range, clustered together in a small area.

There had been five waiters in the range of the shot. Two of the three in the middle found themselves cut in two, their lives ending before they knew what had happened to them. Another two hit the floor with their life ebbing swiftly away, vital organs mashed by the shot and the splintering of bone, shock waves turning human flesh into jelly. The fifth had tried to dive out of the way, and his hip had been shattered by the charge, the bone driving up into his guts and causing a massive internal hemorrhage. But he was still conscious, and pulled his P-38 free as Stamp swung around the muzzle of the shotgun and fired again. He was about to shoot when a chatter of SMG fire inscribed a line from the waiter's throat to hip, ending his chances of fighting back.

Sugarman let up on the pressure he'd placed on the Uzi's trigger, and moved the gun around to back Stamp's play.

Only three waiters were on this side of the door, but they had the time to break rank and try to dive for safety. So the charge only took out one, the guy in the middle, and unsure which way to dive, he had only succeeded in bringing his chest and head in line with the majority of the charge. What had once been human was instantly reduced to a sack of blood and dead flesh.

As they went down, they managed to snap off shots at Stamp, but the big man had the luck of fortune favoring the brave, the 9 mm shells from the P-38s flying high and wide.

They had no chance to try to take a better aim: Sugarman sprayed them with fire from the Uzi, keeping his fingers tapped on the trigger as he arced the SMG from one to the other, spending some ammo on the already pulped waiter in the center of his field of fire.

The charge from the first blast, slowed as it had been by the yielding flesh and bone of the targets, had still managed to make an impression on the closed doors, splintering the wood. The second blast, the majority of which hadn't hit a human target, hit the doors full on, giving short shrift to the lock that kept them closed. Blasted out of its mooring, the force of the separation pushed the doors open, revealing to the two men outside the sight of Bolan and King diving to the floor.

WHEN THE FIRST SHOTGUN blast exploded, everyone in the room except for the soldier was momentarily stunned.

Bolan, however, had other ideas. He threw himself to his right, at the same time reaching out to his left and pushing Traci King away from him.

"Down!" he yelled.

She needed no repeat of the order, allowing the momentum from Bolan's hand to aid her own dive.

The soldier's yell snapped the Chinese out of their sudden surprise, and as the second blast blew the doors open, the enforcers directed their fire toward their two prisoners, and also blindly towards the doors.

It was this division of fire that gave Bolan and King the chance they needed to make some kind of cover. Against a blanket of fire, they would almost certainly have been hit.

Bolan came out of the roll underneath a table, the top of it chopped by a succession of bullets, splinters raining around him, the tablecloth shredded by the fire. He pulled the table over so that it formed a shield—however ineffectual—and came up above the top of this shield with the Beretta in one hand and the Desert Eagle in another. The immediate source of danger was at the two doorways to the kitchens, where the waiters and cooks with MP-5s were clustered. Taking initial aim at the nearest group, the soldier gently tapped the trigger of the Beretta, shots chopping into the cluster of gunmen and immobilizing them.

Across the room from him, King had decided to deal with the enforcers clustered around Lin Ho. She wanted to leave the head of the triad alive if possible, as she had a few questions about her sister that she wanted to put to him, now that Sartini was dead. The four enforcers had spread out and were adopting defensive positions. Lin Ho was still upright, firing the Browning Hi-Power toward the door.

She heard a yell from behind her, more a roar, if truth be told. Stamp leveled the M-4000, high on pain and adrenaline, bullets from the Browning thudding into the wall around him. One hit him in the thigh, but he was so high on the buzz of action that he seemed not to notice. Instead, it just acted as the spur for him to fire, the shotgun exploding in his grasp.

The shot wasn't accurate, but the spread of the shot from the shotgun was enough to make it so. The window behind the triad chief exploded into a crystallized shower of glass that rained down onto the street below, pulverized by the bulk of the M-4000s load.

The glass rain was also joined by a fine mist of blood, flesh and splintered bone. The charge caught Lin Ho on his right-hand side. The triad chief spun in a complete circle, the high, keening yell of his agony cutting through the sound of gun-fire.

He was still alive when he spun, out of control, through the empty space created by the shattered window, tumbling down three floors to land on the sidewalk below.

If he had survived the blast, then there was no way he would survive the fall.

Sugarman cast a worried glance toward Stamp. The pain had just cut through the big man's endorphins, and he stag-gered back against the wall, almost dropping the M-4000, sinking to one side as his thigh gave way under the injury. Sugarman knew he would have to help his partner get the hell out, but first there were other matters to attend to.

Belasko seemed to have one group of gunmen pinned down, and was picking them off with ease, but those shel-tering by the other kitchen door were still able to fire at will. Well, it was Sugarman's turn to show what he was made of. Switching the Uzi to continuous fire and keeping it braced against his hip, Sugarman directed it toward the area inhab-ited by the gunmen and tapped the trigger, keeping his fin-ger down as he sprayed an arc across the doorway.

The Chinese tried to take cover—some scrambled back toward the door and into the shelter of the kitchens—but there wasn't enough time for them to effect such a maneu-ver as the hail of fire chopped into them, cutting them down. The door to their rear was blown back on its hinges by the force of Sugarman's assault.

With the gunmen down, Sugarman moved across to his partner. Stamp was breathing heavily through his mouth, but was still grinning like a maniac.

"Jesus, Dan, I can't remember the last time I had so much fun. Joke, dude, joke," he added, seeing his partner's bemused expression. "I think we need to get out, and quick. This isn't a private fight, not now that laughing boy's hit the road."

"Shut up and grab hold," Sugarman gruffly ordered, offering his arm and shoulder for the big man's support. He knew that Stamp was right, and that they needed to find a way out before the police caught up with them.

Meanwhile, there were still four enforcers to deal with. They had taken cover and were firing at whatever targets they could find. King fired a few rounds from the CZ-75 at them, but knew that picking them off would be harder now they had cover. It would take time, and that was the one thing they didn't have.

Since their cover was already blown—along with half the frontage of the restaurant—then maybe a little more mayhem might act as a cover, as well as finishing off the opposition. She put her hand into the bag and came up with the last of the antipersonnel grenades that she had been carrying. She flipped the pin, let the spoon up and lobbed the bomb in a gentle arc toward the window.

It hit one of the tables and bounced with a dull clunk onto the floor, slap-bang in the middle of the spread of four enforcers. They yelled at one another, trying to move away. But there wasn't time, and the press of tables that had afforded them cover now acted only as an obstruction.

"Fire in the hole!" she yelled before the grenade detonated.

The shockwave took out the remaining glass, the blast making the walls of the dining room shake, plaster showering down on them in a fine powder. The fragmentation grenade made quick work of the four enforcers, the shards of metal packed tightly inside the explosive shredding flesh and splintering bone. Some of the metal blew out over the streets, harmless by the time it rained down on the onlookers below.

Bolan and King hunkered down behind their makeshift shelters, hoping they would hold. Just as Stamp got to his feet, Sugarman pushed him down again, falling on top of him to try to effectively shelter the wounded man from the blast.

Thankfully, both their jaws had fallen open at the sudden action, so they were spared the eardrum-bursting change in pressure. Bolan and King had been prepared, but the two private eyes weren't used to operating with grenades, and it was only luck that saved them.

A luck that would have to hold if they were going to get out of there without being arrested or shot down by the police.

Bolan was on his feet before the others. Scanning the area, he could see that all enemy gunmen were down, and their way was clear to effect evacuation. The only problem was how.

"Come on, let's move," he said, checking King and then Stamp and Sugarman. The woman was already on her feet, having reached into her bag and pulled out the AKSU, ready for anything that would be thrown at her.

She was shaping up into one hell of a fighter, Bolan thought as he moved across to the two private eyes. Sugarman was on his feet and was helping Stamp upright. The big man was in pain, and the thigh wound was bleeding heavily.

"Not been your day, has it?" Bolan said as he hastily bound the wound. He then took Stamp by his free arm, so that both he and Sugarman could aid the big man. "We need evac, and now. There has to be a back way, but we don't know who'll be around. Traci, take point, and stay alert."

"I haven't come this far to get killed or taken because I'm stupid," she said. "Come on..."

Stamp still held the M-4000 in the hand that was draped over Bolan's shoulder, and although he was limping heavily he was still managing to keep pace. With their free hands, the soldier and the detective held the Beretta and the Uzi respectively.

King took the door, AKSU arcing around for danger, and then took them through the kitchen to the service stairs that led down to the ground floor at the rear of the restaurant.

It was deserted, although she didn't let up vigilance for a moment, they were able to descend rapidly until they were at the rear entrance.

After the explosion and the gunfire, and knowing that their chief was dead on the sidewalk outside the restaurant, the remaining triad enforcers in the restaurant had to have decided that it was a better move to retreat and await orders from a higher authority than to hang around and get arrested. Certainly, the sirens were alarmingly near.

At the rear of the restaurant was an alleyway filled with trash cans that overflowed. At each end was a small side road, busy in the nighttime rush and the panic engendered by the firefight. Bolan knew that taking either wasn't an option, but how else could they make an effective escape?

Opposite the restaurant's rear exit was a similar doorway for what could have been a similar restaurant. But this was in darkness, suggesting the business was closed.

"We'll go through if it's empty, see where it takes us," Bolan said, indicating the door.

King agreed, understanding what Bolan required. As they approached the exit doors, she used the stock of the AKSU to break the glass on the double doors, reaching through carefully to slip the bolt and thumb the lock keeping it shut, not wanting to rip open her arm on the jagged glass.

The door opened, and Bolan and Sugarman led Stamp inside. King followed and closed the doors, hoping the broken glass wouldn't be immediately apparent. They only needed a few minutes' leeway.

The building had either been a restaurant that was being refurbished, or was about to be one. There were signs of building work and redecoration, which no doubt accounted for the ease with which they had been able to gain access. Moving to the front part of the building, they could see that it gave fronted a busy street.

"How about up?" Bolan queried.

He turned to the big man. "Justin, would these buildings be linked by a walkway, like the club last night?"

Stamp nodded. "More than likely."

"Okay, we need to check that out," the soldier said, searching for the staircase. Even in the darkness, there was enough ambient light from the street filtering through for them to find it with ease, and although Stamp was beginning to find stair climbing difficult, they managed to reach the roof quickly.

It was as the soldier had suspected. The walkways led along the length of the block, and fire escapes were placed at strategic points along the length, taking them down into the street.

"We can stay up here for a while. I don't figure they'll be looking here just yet. But we need to get the car, and quickly."

Sugarman screwed up his face into something that may have been a wry smile. "That'll have to be me, Mike. The rest of us are far too conspicuous. At least I'm not covered in sewage or blood. But where the hell are you going to meet me?"

Bolan looked out over the street below. On the far side of the block, police were starting to move slowly down the alley. The front of Hoo Hing had to be teeming with them. From the way they moved, they were assuming that there were still hostile forces inside. A thorough search of the restaurant might buy them time.

"Let me worry about that," Bolan told them. "You take the end building, go down through there. I can see light from the front on the street below, so the business should be open, easy to get out. Get the car, bring it back here quick and drive down the road slowly. I'll keep a lookout for you, and just be ready to move. How long?"

Sugarman shrugged. "About ten from here. Can't guarantee faster with the police and the traffic."

Bolan cursed to himself. It would be cutting things a little too fine.

"Okay, Danny, just do your best with it," he said, clapping the man on the shoulder. "Go..."

SUGARMAN MADE the end building and entered the top floor. It was a strip club, and he had to pass through the dressing rooms and down through the auditorium to get out. He kept his hand on the P-38 in his pocket in case he had to deal with any of the bouncers on his way, but fortunately it wasn't a triad-controlled club; any Maltese or hired bouncers were too slow, too perplexed by where he had sprung from to challenge him effectively. It was with a sigh of relief that he left the front of the building and crossed over the road, circling around the police barriers erected along the road outside the restaurant. Sparing it the briefest of glances, he could see the front of the building had a huge hole where the third floor should be, and the sidewalk below was covered in blood and a tarpaulin, where Lin Ho's body lay.

It took five minutes to reach the car. It hadn't been towed or ticketed, and it wasn't boxed in. Sugarman slipped behind the wheel and keyed the ignition.

He pulled out into the traffic, which was slowed by the closure of the roads around the restaurant, but not gridlocked as the police were keeping the roads fluid for their own vehicles.

He just had to pray he wasn't stopped.

"HE'S HERE. Let's do it," Bolan said as he saw Sugarman[s car turn into the road below them, slowing as it cornered.

"You up to this, sweetie?" King asked Stamp. While Bolan had kept watch, she had been tending the big man's wounded thigh. The bullet had passed through, and although the bleeding had been staunched, it still needed to be cleaned and closed professionally.

Another job for Tyler, if they got back to Sugarman's in one piece.

"Yeah, I reckon I can do it," Stamp said as she helped him to his feet. "'Specially if you keep calling me 'sweetie,'" he added with a grin.

"Okay, we go back down through here," Stamp said, turning to the building through which they had ascended.

It presented the best solution under the circumstances. As it was deserted, they wouldn't draw attention to themselves. And it was at the far end of the road from where Sugarman's car currently crawled, giving them—in theory—enough time to get down to the ground floor before he reached them.

Bolan took the stairs three at a time, checking that King and Stamp weren't falling too far behind. By the time he was at the closed and bolted front of the restaurant, all white-washed glass, they were on the final flight.

The locks on the door were simple for him to slip. He pulled the door open, risking a glance down the road.

Sugarman's car was nearly on them. Bolan turned to the others as they came up close.

"Now—quick as possible," he directed.

Bolan slipped out of the door. Sugarman saw him and pulled into the curb. He unlocked the back door, which the Executioner pulled open, leaving it for King to help in Stamp as the soldier moved around to slip into the passenger seat.

It took only a couple of seconds, but they seemed an eternity.

"Go," Bolan growled as the doors clicked shut.

Sugarman pulled smoothly away from the curb and eased into the traffic.

"It's hell by Hoo Hing, but if I take us this way we should avoid any roadblocks," Sugarman said in a strained voice. "At least, I hope so."

He was right. The traffic was heavy, but the police presence was concentrated on the northern end of Soho, while Sugarman headed south and opted to take a road leading to the south of the Thames.

They drove for nearly two hours, Sugarman taking them over two bridges and crisscrossing the river to shake any possible tail, leave a false trail if they had been spotted and evade any roadblocks that might have been laid. Eventually they reached Sugarman's home.

Bolan and King helped Stamp to settle comfortably, while Sugarman calmed his wife. "Steph, I'll explain it later. First I've got to get Tyler back here."

While Sugarman was on the phone, King turned to Bolan.

"You know, I should feel good about getting rid of those bastards, but I don't. It hasn't got me any nearer finding Elena."

"Or poor little Sammi," Stamp added.

"I know what it's like to lose someone close," Bolan said to the woman. "I've lost too many to count. But if they're gone, the only thing you can do is stop it happening to someone else, to someone else's sister. I don't feel good about it, either, but it's a job that has to be done. Speaking of which..."

He took the phone from Sugarman, who told them Tyler was on his way. Bolan then dialed a number that he knew would pass through several cutouts before it reached a secure line, and waited for the pickup.

"Morning, Hal," he said neutrally.

"Striker! Where the hell are you?" growled Hal Brognola, whose morning had taken both a turn for the better and the worse with this call. "No, maybe you don't have to answer that," he added. "We've seen CNN on what's been going down in London. I assume you're involved?"

"You know me. I just can't let something slide," Bolan answered in a good-natured tone. "I need a flight to replace the one I missed...and I need a little favor."

"Tell me why I don't like the sound of that," Brognola commented warily.

"I need you to get in touch with your contact in British intelligence. You have to vouch for three people."

The Executioner knew that the big Fed would go out on a limb to help him. Traci, Justin and Danny deserved a break.

They'd laid it on the line for him, and he had to make sure they'd be free of scrutiny by the law.

His War Everlasting had taken an odd turn here in London, but a score had been settled, a blood debt paid. It was the least he could do for the innocents.

DEATH LANDS®

Bloodfire

Available in December 2003
at your favorite retail outlet.

Hearing a rumor that The Trader, his old teacher and friend, is still alive, Ryan and his warrior group struggle across the Texas desert to find the truth. But an enemy with a score to settle is in hot pursuit—and so is the elusive Trader. And so the stage is set for a showdown between mortal enemies, where the scales of revenge and death will be balanced with brutal finality.

James Axler
Outlanders®

AWAKENING

Cryogenically preserved before the nukes obliterated their own way of life, an elite team of battle-hardened American fighting men has now been reactivated. Their first mission in a tortured new world: move in and secure Cerberus Redoubt and the mat-trans network at any cost. In a world where trust is hard won and harder kept, Kane and his fellow exiles must convince Team Phoenix that they are on the same side—for humanity, and against the hybrids and their willing human allies.

In the Outlands, the shocking truth is humanity's last hope.